Weir of Hermiston by Robert

Weir of Hermiston by Robert

TO MY WIFE

I saw rain falling and the rainbow drawn

On Lammermuir. Hearkening I heard again

In my precipitous city beaten bells

Winnow the keen sea wind. And here afar,

Intent on my own race and place, I wrote.

Take thou the writing: thine it is. For who

Burnished the sword, blew on the drowsy coal,

Held still the target higher, chary of praise

And prodigal of counsel - who but thou?

So now, in the end, if this the least be good,

If any deed be done, if any fire

Burn in the imperfect page, the praise be thine.

INTRODUCTORY

IN the wild end of a moorland parish, far out of the sight of any house, there stands a cairn among the heather, and a little by east of it, in the going down of the brae-side, a monument with some verses half defaced. It was here that Claverhouse shot with his own hand the Praying Weaver of Balweary, and the chisel of Old Mortality has clinked on that lonely gravestone. Public and domestic history have thus marked with a bloody finger this hollow among the hills; and since the Cameronian gave his life there, two hundred years ago, in a glorious folly, and without comprehension or regret, the silence of the moss has been broken once again by the report of firearms and the cry of the dying.

The Deil's Hags was the old name. But the place is now called Francie's Cairn. For a while it was told that Francie walked. Aggic Hogg met him in the gloaming by the cairnside, and he spoke to her, with chattering teeth, so that his words were lost. He pursued Rob Todd (if any one could have believed Robbie) for the space of half a mile with pitiful entreaties. But the age is one of incredulity; these superstitious decorations speedily fell off; and the facts of the story itself, like the bones of a giant buried there and half dug up, survived, naked and imperfect, in the memory of the scattered neighbours. To this day, of winter nights, when the sleet is on the window and the cattle are quiet page 2 / 166

in the byre, there will be told again, amid the silence of the young and the additions and corrections of the old, the tale of the Justice-Clerk and of his son, young Hermiston, that vanished from men's knowledge; of the two Kirsties and the Four Black Brothers of the Cauldstaneslap; and of Frank Innes, "the young fool advocate," that came into these moorland parts to find his destiny.

CHAPTER I - LIFE AND DEATH OF MRS. WEIR

THE Lord Justice-Clerk was a stranger in that part of the country; but his lady wife was known there from a child, as her race had been before her. The old "riding Rutherfords of Hermiston," of whom she was the last descendant, had been famous men of yore, ill neighbours, ill subjects, and ill husbands to their wives though not their properties.

Tales of them were rife for twenty miles about; and their name was even printed in the page of our Scots histories, not always to their credit.

One bit the dust at Flodden; one was hanged at his peel door by James the Fifth; another fell dead in a carouse with Tom Dalyell; while a fourth (and that was Jean's own father) died presiding at a Hell-Fire Club, of which he was the founder. There were many heads shaken in Crossmichael at that judgment; the more so as the man had a villainous reputation among high and low, and both with the godly and the worldly.

At that very hour of his demise, he had ten going pleas before the Session, eight of them oppressive. And the same doom extended even to his agents; his grieve, that had been his right hand in many a left-hand business, being cast from his horse one night and drowned in a peat-hag on the Kye-skairs; and his very doer (although lawyers have long spoons) page 3 / 166

surviving him not long, and dying on a sudden in a bloody flux.

In all these generations, while a male Rutherford was in the saddle with his lads, or brawling in a change-house, there would be always a white-faced wife immured at home in the old peel or the later mansion-house.

It seemed this succession of martyrs bided long, but took their vengeance in the end, and that was in the person of the last descendant, Jean. She bore the name of the

Rutherfords, but she was the daughter of their trembling wives. At the first she was not wholly without charm.

Neighbours recalled in her, as a child, a strain of elfin wilfulness, gentle little mutinies, sad little gaieties, even a morning gleam of beauty that was not to be fulfilled. She withered in the growing, and (whether it was the sins of her sires or the sorrows of her mothers) came to her maturity depressed, and, as it were, defaced; no blood of life in her, no grasp or gaiety; pious, anxious, tender, tearful, and incompetent.

It was a wonder to many that she had married - seeming so wholly of the stuff that makes old maids. But chance cast her in the path of Adam Weir, then the new Lord-Advocate, a recognised, risen man, the conqueror of many obstacles, and thus late in the day beginning to think upon a wife. He was one who looked rather to obedience than beauty, yet it would seem he was struck with her at the first look. "Wha's she?" he said, turning to his host; and, when he had been told, "Ay," says he,

"she looks menseful. She minds me - "; and then, after a pause (which some have been daring enough to set down to sentimental recollections),

"Is she releegious?" he asked, and was shortly after, at his own page 4 / 166

request, presented. The acquaintance, which it seems profane to call a courtship, was pursued with Mr. Weir's accustomed industry, and was long a legend, or rather a source of legends, in the Parliament House. He was described coming, rosy with much port, into the drawing-room, walking direct up to the lady, and assailing her with pleasantries, to which the embarrassed fair one responded, in what seemed a kind of agony, "Eh, Mr. Weir!" or "O,

Mr. Weir!" or "Keep me, Mr. Weir!" On the very eve of their engagement, it was related that one had drawn near to the tender couple, and had overheard the lady cry out, with the tones of one who talked for the sake of talking, "Keep me, Mr. Weir, and what became of him?" and the profound accents of the suitor reply, "Haangit, mem, haangit." The motives upon either side were much debated. Mr.

Weir must have supposed his bride to be somehow suitable; perhaps he belonged to that class of men who think a weak head the ornament of women - an opinion invariably punished in this life. Her descent and her estate were beyond question. Her wayfaring ancestors and her litigious father had done well by Jean. There was ready money and there were broad acres, ready to fall wholly to the husband, to lend dignity to his descendants, and to himself a title, when he should be called upon the Bench. On the side of Jean, there was perhaps some fascination of curiosity as to this unknown male animal that approached her with the roughness of a ploughman and the APLOMB of an advocate. Being so trenchantly opposed to all she knew, loved, or understood, he may well have seemed to her the extreme, if scarcely the ideal, of his sex. And besides, he was an ill man to refuse. A little over forty at the period of his marriage, he looked already older, and to the force of manhood added the senatorial dignity of years; it was, perhaps, with an unreverend awe, but he was awful. The Bench, the Bar, and the most

experienced and reluctant witness, bowed to his authority - and why not Jeannie Rutherford?

The heresy about foolish women is always punished, I have said, and Lord Hermiston began to pay the penalty at once. His house in George Square was wretchedly ill-guided; nothing answerable to the expense of maintenance but the cellar, which was his own private care. When things went wrong at dinner, as they continually did, my lord would look up the table at his wife: "I think these broth would be better to sweem in than to sup." Or else to the butler: "Here, M'Killop, awa' wi' this Raadical gigot - tak' it to the French, man, and bring me some puddocks! It seems rather a sore kind of a business that I should be all day in Court haanging Raadicals, and get nawthing to my denner." Of course this was but a manner of speaking, and he had never hanged a man for being a Radical in his life; the law, of which he was the faithful minister, directing otherwise. And of course these growls were in the nature of pleasantry, but it was of a recondite sort; and uttered as they were in his resounding voice, and commented on by that expression which they called in the Parliament House "Hermiston's hanging face" - they struck mere dismay into the wife. She sat before him speechless and fluttering; at each dish, as at a fresh ordeal, her eye hovered toward my lord's countenance and fell again; if he but ate in silence, unspeakable relief was her portion; if there were complaint, the world was darkened. She would seek out the cook, who was always her SISTER IN

THE LORD. "O, my dear, this is the most dreidful thing that my lord can never be contented in his own house!" she would begin; and weep and pray with the cook; and then the cook would pray with Mrs. Weir; and the next page 6 / 166

day's meal would never be a penny the better - and the next cook (when she came) would be worse, if anything, but just as pious. It was often wondered that Lord Hermiston bore it as he did; indeed, he was a stoical old voluptuary, contented with sound wine and plenty of it. But there were moments when he overflowed. Perhaps half a dozen times in the history of his married life - "Here! tak' it awa', and bring me a piece bread and kebbuck!" he had exclaimed, with an appalling explosion of his voice and rare gestures. None thought to dispute or to make excuses; the service was arrested; Mrs. Weir sat at the head of the table whimpering without disguise; and his lordship opposite munched his bread and cheese in ostentatious disregard. Once only, Mrs. Weir had ventured to appeal. He was passing her chair on his way into the study.

"O, Edom!" she wailed, in a voice tragic with tears, and reaching out to him both hands, in one of which she held a sopping pocket-handkerchief.

He paused and looked upon her with a face of wrath, into which there stole, as he looked, a twinkle of humour.

"Noansense!" he said. "You and your noansense! What do I want with a Christian faim'ly? I want Christian broth! Get me a lass that can plain-boil a potato, if she was a whure off the streets." And with these words, which echoed in her tender ears like blasphemy, he had passed on to his study and shut the door behind him.

Such was the housewifery in George Square. It was better at Hermiston, page 7 / 166

where Kirstie Elliott, the sister of a neighbouring bonnet-laird, and an eighteenth cousin of the lady's, bore the charge of all, and kept a trim house and a good country table. Kirstie was a woman in a thousand, clean, capable, notable; once a moorland Helen, and still comely as a blood horse and healthy as the hill wind. High in flesh and voice and colour, she ran the house with her whole intemperate soul, in a bustle, not without buffets. Scarce more pious than decency in those days required, she was the cause of many an anxious thought and many a tearful prayer to Mrs. Weir. Housekeeper and mistress renewed the parts of Martha and Mary; and though with a pricking conscience, Mary reposed on Martha's strength as on a rock. Even Lord Hermiston held Kirstie in a particular regard. There were few with whom he unbent so gladly, few whom he favoured with so many pleasantries. "Kirstie and me maun have our joke," he would declare in high good-humour, as he buttered Kirstie's scones, and she waited at table. A man who had no need either of love or of popularity, a keen reader of men and of events, there was perhaps only one truth for which he was quite unprepared: he would have been quite unprepared to learn that Kirstie hated him. He thought maid and master were well matched; hard, bandy, healthy, broad Scots folk, without a hair of nonsense to the pair of them. And the fact was that she made a goddess and an only child of the effete and tearful lady; and even as she waited at table her hands would sometimes itch for my lord's ears.

Thus, at least, when the family were at Hermiston, not only my lord, but Mrs. Weir too, enjoyed a holiday. Free from the dreadful looking-for of the miscarried dinner, she would mind her seam, read her piety books, page 8 / 166

and take her walk (which was my lord's orders), sometimes by herself, sometimes with Archie, the only child of that scarce natural union. The child was her next bond to life. Her frosted sentiment bloomed again, she breathed deep of life, she let loose her heart, in that society.

The miracle of her motherhood was ever new to her. The sight of the little man at her skirt intoxicated her with the sense of power, and froze her with the consciousness of her responsibility. She looked forward, and, seeing him in fancy grow up and play his diverse part on the world's theatre, caught in her breath and lifted up her courage with a lively effort. It was only with the child that she forgot herself and was at moments natural; yet it was only with the child that she had conceived and managed to pursue a scheme of conduct. Archie was to be a great man and a good; a minister if possible, a saint for certain. She tried to engage his mind upon her favourite books, Rutherford's LETTERS, Scougalls GRACE ABOUNDING, and the like. It was a common practice of hers (and strange to remember now) that she would carry the child to the Deil's Hags, sit with him on the Praying Weaver's stone, and talk of the Covenanters till their tears ran down. Her view of history was wholly artless, a design in snow and ink; upon the one side, tender innocents with psalms upon their lips; upon the other, the persecutors, booted, bloody-minded, flushed with wine: a suffering Christ, a raging Beelzebub. PERSECUTOR was a word that knocked upon the woman's heart; it was her highest thought of wickedness, and the mark of it was on her house. Her great-great-grandfather had drawn the sword against the Lord's anointed on the field of Rullion Green, and breathed his last (tradition said) in the arms of the detestable Dalyell. Nor could she blind herself to this, that had they lived in those old days, Hermiston himself would have been numbered alongside of Bloody MacKenzie and the

politic Lauderdale and Rothes, in the band of God's immediate enemies.

The sense of this moved her to the more fervour; she had a voice for that name of PERSECUTOR that thrilled in the child's marrow; and when one day the mob hooted and hissed them all in my lord's travelling carriage, and cried, "Down with the persecutor! down with Hanging Hermiston!" and mamma covered her eyes and wept, and papa let down the glass and looked out upon the rabble with his droll formidable face, bitter and smiling, as they said he sometimes looked when he gave sentence, Archie was for the moment too much amazed to be alarmed, but he had scarce got his mother by herself before his shrill voice was raised demanding an explanation: why had they called papa a persecutor?

"Keep me, my precious!" she exclaimed. "Keep me, my dear! this is poleetical. Ye must never ask me anything poleetical, Erchie. Your faither is a great man, my dear, and it's no for me or you to be judging him. It would be telling us all, if we behaved ourselves in our several stations the way your faither does in his high office; and let me hear no more of any such disrespectful and undutiful questions! No that you meant to be undutiful, my lamb; your mother kens that - she kens it well, dearie!" And so slid off to safer topics, and left on the mind of the child an obscure but ineradicable sense of something wrong.

Mrs. Weir's philosophy of life was summed in one expression -

tenderness. In her view of the universe, which was all lighted up with a glow out of the doors of hell, good people must walk there in a kind of ecstasy of tenderness. The beasts and plants had no souls; they were here but for a day, and let their day pass gently! And as for the page 10 / 166

immortal men, on what black, downward path were many of them wending, and to what a horror of an immortality! "Are not two sparrows,"

"Whosoever shall smite thee," "God sendeth His rain," "Judge not, that ye be not judged" - these texts made her body of divinity; she put them on in the morning with her clothes and lay down to sleep with them at night; they haunted her like a favourite air, they clung about her like a favourite perfume. Their minister was a marrowy expounder of the law, and my lord sat under him with relish; but Mrs. Weir respected him from far off; heard him (like the cannon of a beleaguered city) usefully booming outside on the dogmatic ramparts; and meanwhile, within and out of shot, dwelt in her private garden which she watered with grateful tears. It seems strange to say of this colourless and ineffectual woman, but she was a true enthusiast, and might have made the sunshine and the glory of a cloister. Perhaps none but Archie knew she could be eloquent; perhaps none but he had seen her - her colour raised, her hands clasped or quivering - glow with gentle ardour. There is a corner of the policy of Hermiston, where you come suddenly in view of the summit of Black Fell, sometimes like the mere grass top of a hill, sometimes (and this is her own expression) like a precious jewel in the heavens. On such days, upon the sudden view of it, her hand would tighten on the child's fingers, her voice rise like a song. "I TO THE

HILLS!" she would repeat. "And O, Erchie, are nae these like the hills of Naphtali?" and her tears would flow.

Upon an impressionable child the effect of this continual and pretty accompaniment to life was deep. The woman's quietism and piety passed on to his different nature undiminished; but whereas in her it was a

native sentiment, in him it was only an implanted dogma. Nature and the child's pugnacity at times revolted. A cad from the Potterrow once struck him in the mouth; he struck back, the pair fought it out in the back stable lane towards the Meadows, and Archie returned with a considerable decline in the number of his front teeth, and unregenerately boasting of the losses of the foe. It was a sore day for Mrs. Weir; she wept and prayed over the infant backslider until my lord was due from Court, and she must resume that air of tremulous composure with which she always greeted him. The judge was that day in an observant mood, and remarked upon the absent teeth.

"I am afraid Erchie will have been fechting with some of they blagyard lads," said Mrs. Weir.

My lord's voice rang out as it did seldom in the privacy of his own house. "I'll have norm of that, sir!" he cried. "Do you hear me? -

nonn of that! No son of mine shall be speldering in the glaur with any dirty raibble."

The anxious mother was grateful for so much support; she had even feared the contrary. And that night when she put the child to bed - "Now, my dear, ye see!" she said, "I told you what your faither would think of it, if he heard ye had fallen into this dreidful sin; and let you and me pray to God that ye may be keepit from the like temptation or strengthened to resist it!"

The womanly falsity of this was thrown away. Ice and iron cannot be welded; and the points of view of the Justice-Clerk and Mrs. Weir were not less unassimilable. The character and position of his father had long been a stumbling-block to Archie, and with every year of his age the difficulty grew more instant. The man was mostly silent; when he spoke at all, it was to speak of the things of the world, always in a worldly spirit, often in language that the child had been schooled to think coarse, and sometimes with words that he knew to be sins in themselves. Tenderness was the first duty, and my lord was invariably harsh. God was love; the name of my lord (to all who knew him) was fear. In the world, as schematised for Archie by his mother, the place was marked for such a creature. There were some whom it was good to pity and well (though very likely useless) to pray for; they were named reprobates, goats, God's enemies, brands for the burning; and Archie tallied every mark of identification, and drew the inevitable private inference that the Lord Justice-Clerk was the chief of sinners.

The mother's honesty was scarce complete. There was one influence she feared for the child and still secretly combated; that was my lord's; and half unconsciously, half in a wilful blindness, she continued to undermine her husband with his son. As long as Archie remained silent, she did so ruthlessly, with a single eye to heaven and the child's salvation; but the day came when Archie spoke. It was 1801, and Archie was seven, and beyond his years for curiosity and logic, when he brought the case up openly. If judging were sinful and forbidden, how came papa to be a judge? to have that sin for a trade? to bear the name of it for a distinction?

page 13 / 166

"I can't see it," said the little Rabbi, and wagged his head.

Mrs. Weir abounded in commonplace replies.

"No, I cannae see it," reiterated Archie. "And I'll tell you what, mamma, I don't think you and me's justifeed in staying with him."

The woman awoke to remorse, she saw herself disloyal to her man, her sovereign and bread-winner, in whom (with what she had of worldliness) she took a certain subdued pride. She expatiated in reply on my lord's honour and greatness; his useful services in this world of sorrow and wrong, and the place in which he stood, far above where babes and innocents could hope to see or criticise. But she had builded too well

- Archie had his answers pat: Were not babes and innocents the type of the kingdom of heaven? Were not honour and greatness the badges of the world? And at any rate, how about the mob that had once seethed about the carriage?

"It's all very fine," he concluded, "but in my opinion papa has no right to be it. And it seems that's not the worst yet of it. It seems he's called "The Hanging judge" - it seems he's crooool. I'll tell you what it is, mamma, there's a tex' borne in upon me: It were better for that man if a milestone were bound upon his back and him flung into the deepestmost pairts of the sea."

"O, my lamb, ye must never say the like of that!" she cried. "Ye're to honour faither and mother, dear, that your days may be long in the land.

It's Atheists that cry out against him - French Atheists, Erchie! Ye would never surely even yourself down to be saying the same thing as French Atheists? It would break my heart to think that of you. And O, Erchie, here are'na YOU setting up to JUDGE? And have ye no forgot God's plain command - the First with Promise, dear? Mind you upon the beam and the mote!"

Having thus carried the war into the enemy's camp, the terrified lady breathed again. And no doubt it is easy thus to circumvent a child with catchwords, but it may be questioned how far it is effectual. An instinct in his breast detects the quibble, and a voice condemns it. He will instantly submit, privately hold the same opinion. For even in this simple and antique relation of the mother and the child, hypocrisies are multiplied.

When the Court rose that year and the family returned to Hermiston, it was a common remark in all the country that the lady was sore failed.

She seemed to loose and seize again her touch with life, now sitting inert in a sort of durable bewilderment, anon waking to feverish and weak activity. She dawdled about the lasses at their work, looking stupidly on; she fell to rummaging in old cabinets and presses, and desisted when half through; she would begin remarks with an air of animation and drop them without a struggle. Her common appearance was page 15 / 166

of one who has forgotten something and is trying to remember; and when she overhauled, one after another, the worthless and touching mementoes of her youth, she might have been seeking the clue to that lost thought.

During this period, she gave many gifts to the neighbours and house lasses, giving them with a manner of regret that embarrassed the recipients.

The last night of all she was busy on some female work, and toiled upon it with so manifest and painful a devotion that my lord (who was not often curious) inquired as to its nature.

She blushed to the eyes. "O, Edom, it's for you!" she said. "It's slippers. I - I hae never made ye any."

"Ye daft auld wife!" returned his lordship. "A bonny figure I would be, palmering about in bauchles!"

The next day, at the hour of her walk, Kirstie interfered. Kirstie took this decay of her mistress very hard; bore her a grudge, quarrelled with and railed upon her, the anxiety of a genuine love wearing the disguise of temper. This day of all days she insisted disrespectfully, with rustic fury, that Mrs. Weir should stay at home. But, "No, no," she said, "it's my lord's orders," and set forth as usual. Archie was visible in the acre bog, engaged upon some childish enterprise, the instrument of which was mire; and she stood and looked at him a while like one about to call; then thought otherwise, sighed, and shook her page 16 / 166

head, and proceeded on her rounds alone. The house lasses were at the burnside washing, and saw her pass with her loose, weary, dowdy gait.

"She's a terrible feckless wife, the mistress!" said the one.

"Tut," said the other, "the wumman's seeck."

"Weel, I canna see nae differ in her," returned the first. "A fushionless quean, a feckless carline."

The poor creature thus discussed rambled a while in the grounds without a purpose. Tides in her mind ebbed and flowed, and carried her to and fro like seaweed. She tried a path, paused, returned, and tried another; questing, forgetting her quest; the spirit of choice extinct in her bosom, or devoid of sequency. On a sudden, it appeared as though she had remembered, or had formed a resolution, wheeled about, returned with hurried steps, and appeared in the dining-room, where Kirstie was at the cleaning, like one charged with an important errand.

"Kirstie!" she began, and paused; and then with conviction, "Mr. Weir isna speeritually minded, but he has been a good man to me."

It was perhaps the first time since her husband's elevation that she had forgotten the handle to his name, of which the tender, inconsistent woman was not a little proud. And when Kirstie looked up at the page 17 / 166

speaker's face, she was aware of a change.

"Godsake, what's the maitter wi' ye, mem?" cried the housekeeper, starting from the rug.

"I do not ken," answered her mistress, shaking her head. "But he is not speeritually minded, my dear."

"Here, sit down with ye! Godsake, what ails the wife?" cried Kirstie, and helped and forced her into my lord's own chair by the cheek of the hearth.

"Keep me, what's this?" she gasped. "Kirstie, what's this? I'm frich'ened."

They were her last words.

It was the lowering nightfall when my lord returned. He had the sunset in his back, all clouds and glory; and before him, by the wayside, spied Kirstie Elliott waiting. She was dissolved in tears, and addressed him in the high, false note of barbarous mourning, such as still lingers modified among Scots heather.

"The Lord peety ye, Hermiston! the Lord prepare ye!" she keened out.

page 18 / 166

"Weary upon me, that I should have to tell it!"

He reined in his horse and looked upon her with the hanging face.

"Has the French landit?" cried he.

"Man, man," she said, "is that a' ye can think of? The Lord prepare ye: the Lord comfort and support ye!"

"Is onybody deid?" said his lordship. "It's no Erchie?"

"Bethankit, no!" exclaimed the woman, startled into a more natural tone.

"Na, na, it's no sae bad as that. It's the mistress, my lord; she just fair flittit before my e'en. She just gi'ed a sab and was by wi' it.

Eh, my bonny Miss Jeannie, that I mind sae weel!" And forth again upon that pouring tide of lamentation in which women of her class excel and over-abound.

Lord Hermiston sat in the saddle beholding her. Then he seemed to recover command upon himself.

"Well, it's something of the suddenest," said he. "But she was a dwaibly body from the first."

And he rode home at a precipitate amble with Kirstie at his horse's heels.

Dressed as she was for her last walk, they had laid the dead lady on her bed. She was never interesting in life; in death she was not impressive; and as her husband stood before her, with his hands crossed behind his powerful back, that which he looked upon was the very image of the insignificant.

"Her and me were never cut out for one another," he remarked at last.

"It was a daft-like marriage." And then, with a most unusual gentleness of tone, "Puir bitch," said he, "puir bitch!" Then suddenly: "Where's Erchie?"

Kirstie had decoyed him to her room and given him "a jeely-piece."

"Ye have some kind of gumption, too," observed the judge, and considered his housekeeper grimly. "When all's said," he added, "I micht have done waur - I micht have been marriet upon a skirting Jezebel like you!"

"There's naebody thinking of you, Hermiston!" cried the offended woman.

"We think of her that's out of her sorrows. And could SHE have done waur? Tell me that, Hermiston - tell me that before her clay-cauld corp!"

"Weel, there's some of them gey an' ill to please," observed his lordship.

CHAPTER II - FATHER AND SON

MY Lord Justice-Clerk was known to many; the man Adam Weir perhaps to none. He had nothing to explain or to conceal; he sufficed wholly and silently to himself; and that part of our nature which goes out (too often with false coin) to acquire glory or love, seemed in him to be omitted. He did not try to be loved, he did not care to be; it is probable the very thought of it was a stranger to his mind. He was an admired lawyer, a highly unpopular judge; and he looked down upon those who were his inferiors in either distinction, who were lawyers of less grasp or judges not so much detested. In all the rest of his days and doings, not one trace of vanity appeared; and he went on through life with a mechanical movement, as of the unconscious; that was almost august.

He saw little of his son. In the childish maladies with which the boy was troubled, he would make daily inquiries and daily pay him a visit, entering the sick-room with a facetious and appalling countenance, letting off a few perfunctory jests, and going again swiftly, to the patient's relief. Once, a court holiday falling opportunely, my lord had his carriage, and drove the child himself to Hermiston, the customary place of convalescence. It is conceivable he had been more page 21 / 166

than usually anxious, for that journey always remained in Archie's memory as a thing apart, his father having related to him from beginning to end, and with much detail, three authentic murder cases. Archie went the usual round of other Edinburgh boys, the high school and the college; and Hermiston looked on, or rather looked away, with scarce an affectation of interest in his progress. Daily, indeed, upon a signal after dinner, he was brought in, given nuts and a glass of port, regarded sardonically, sarcastically questioned. "Well, sir, and what have you donn with your book to-day?" my lord might begin, and set him posers in law Latin. To a child just stumbling into Corderius, Papinian and Paul proved quite invincible. But papa had memory of no other. He was not harsh to the little scholar, having a vast fund of patience learned upon the bench, and was at no pains whether to conceal or to express his disappointment. "Well, ye have a long jaunt before ye yet!"

he might observe, yawning, and fall back on his own thoughts (as like as not) until the time came for separation, and my lord would take the decanter and the glass, and be off to the back chamber looking on the Meadows, where he toiled on his cases till the hours were small. There was no "fuller man" on the bench; his memory was marvellous, though wholly legal; if he had to "advise" extempore, none did it better; yet there was none who more earnestly prepared. As he thus watched in the night, or sat at table and forgot the presence of his son, no doubt but he tasted deeply of recondite pleasures. To be wholly devoted to some intellectual exercise is to have succeeded in life; and perhaps only in law and the higher mathematics may this devotion be maintained, suffice to itself without reaction, and find continual rewards without excitement. This atmosphere of his father's sterling industry was the best of Archie's education. Assuredly it did not attract him; assuredly page 22 / 166

it rather rebutted and depressed. Yet it was still present, unobserved like the ticking of a clock, an arid ideal, a tasteless stimulant in the boy's life.

But Hermiston was not all of one piece. He was, besides, a mighty toper; he could sit at wine until the day dawned, and pass directly from the table to the bench with a steady hand and a clear head. Beyond the third bottle, he showed the plebeian in a larger print; the low, gross accent, the low, foul mirth, grew broader and commoner; he became less formidable, and infinitely more disgusting. Now, the boy had inherited from Jean Rutherford a shivering delicacy, unequally mated with potential violence. In the playing-fields, and amongst his own companions, he repaid a coarse expression with a blow; at his father's table (when the time came for him to join these revels) he turned pale and sickened in silence. Of all the guests whom he there encountered, he had toleration for only one: David Keith Carnegie, Lord Glenalmond.

Lord Glenalmond was tall and emaciated, with long features and long delicate hands. He was often compared with the statue of Forbes of Culloden in the Parliament House; and his blue eye, at more than sixty, preserved some of the fire of youth. His exquisite disparity with any of his fellow-guests, his appearance as of an artist and an aristocrat stranded in rude company, riveted the boy's attention; and as curiosity and interest are the things in the world that are the most immediately and certainly rewarded, Lord Glenalmond was attracted by the boy.

"And so this is your son, Hermiston?" he asked, laying his hand on Archie's shoulder. "He's getting a big lad."

"Hout!" said the gracious father, "just his mother over again - daurna say boo to a goose!"

But the stranger retained the boy, talked to him, drew him out, found in him a taste for letters, and a fine, ardent, modest, youthful soul; and encouraged him to be a visitor on Sunday evenings in his bare, cold, lonely dining-room, where he sat and read in the isolation of a bachelor grown old in refinement. The beautiful gentleness and grace of the old judge, and the delicacy of his person, thoughts, and language, spoke to Archie's heart in its own tongue. He conceived the ambition to be such another; and, when the day came for him to choose a profession, it was in emulation of Lord Glenalmond, not of Lord Hermiston, that he chose the Bar. Hermiston looked on at this friendship with some secret pride, but openly with the intolerance of scorn. He scarce lost an opportunity to put them down with a rough jape; and, to say truth, it was not difficult, for they were neither of them quick. He had a word of contempt for the whole crowd of poets, painters, fiddlers, and their admirers, the bastard race of amateurs, which was continually on his lips. "Signor Feedle-eerie!" he would say. "O, for Goad's sake, no more of the Signor!"

"You and my father are great friends, are you not?" asked Archie once.

"There is no man that I more respect, Archie," replied Lord Glenalmond.

"He is two things of price. He is a great lawyer, and he is upright as page 24 / 166

the day."

"You and he are so different," said the boy, his eyes dwelling on those of his old friend, like a lover's on his mistress's.

"Indeed so," replied the judge; "very different. And so I fear are you and he. Yet I would like it very ill if my young friend were to misjudge his father. He has all the Roman virtues: Cato and Brutus were such; I think a son's heart might well be proud of such an ancestry of one."

"And I would sooner he were a plaided herd," cried Archie, with sudden bitterness.

"And that is neither very wise, nor I believe entirely true," returned Glenalmond. "Before you are done you will find some of these expressions rise on you like a remorse. They are merely literary and decorative; they do not aptly express your thought, nor is your thought clearly apprehended, and no doubt your father (if he were here) would say, "Signor Feedle-eerie!"

With the infinitely delicate sense of youth, Archie avoided the subject from that hour. It was perhaps a pity. Had he but talked - talked freely - let himself gush out in words (the way youth loves to do and should), there might have been no tale to write upon the Weirs of page 25 / 166

Hermiston. But the shadow of a threat of ridicule sufficed; in the slight tartness of these words he read a prohibition; and it is likely that Glenalmond meant it so.

Besides the veteran, the boy was without confidant or friend. Serious and eager, he came through school and college, and moved among a crowd of the indifferent, in the seclusion of his shyness. He grew up handsome, with an open, speaking countenance, with graceful, youthful ways; he was clever, he took prizes, he shone in the Speculative Society. It should seem he must become the centre of a crowd of friends; but something that was in part the delicacy of his mother, in part the austerity of his father, held him aloof from all. It is a fact, and a strange one, that among his contemporaries Hermiston's son was thought to be a chip of the old block. "You're a friend of Archie Weir's?" said one to Frank Innes; and Innes replied, with his usual flippancy and more than his usual insight: "I know Weir. but I never met Archie." No one had met Archie, a malady most incident to only sons.

He flew his private signal, and none heeded it; it seemed he was abroad in a world from which the very hope of intimacy was banished; and he looked round about him on the concourse of his fellow-students, and forward to the trivial days and acquaintances that were to come, without hope or interest.

As time went on, the tough and rough old sinner felt himself drawn to the son of his loins and sole continuator of his new family, with softnesses of sentiment that he could hardly credit and was wholly impotent to express. With a face, voice, and manner trained through page 26 / 166

forty years to terrify and repel, Rhadamanthus may be great, but he will scarce be engaging. It is a fact that he tried to propitiate Archie, but a fact that cannot be too lightly taken; the attempt was so unconspicuously made, the failure so stoically supported. Sympathy is not due to these steadfast iron natures. If he failed to gain his son's friendship, or even his son's toleration, on he went up the great, bare staircase of his duty, uncheered and undepressed. There might have been more pleasure in his relations with Archie, so much he may have recognised at moments; but pleasure was a by-product of the singular chemistry of life, which only fools expected.

An idea of Archie's attitude, since we are all grown up and have forgotten the days of our youth, it is more difficult to convey. He made no attempt whatsoever to understand the man with whom he dined and breakfasted. Parsimony of pain, glut of pleasure, these are the two alternating ends of youth; and Archie was of the parsimonious. The wind blew cold out of a certain quarter - he turned his back upon it; stayed as little as was possible in his father's presence; and when there, averted his eyes as much as was decent from his father's face. The lamp shone for many hundred days upon these two at table - my lord, ruddy, gloomy, and unreverent; Archie with a potential brightness that was always dimmed and veiled in that society; and there were not, perhaps, in Christendom two men more radically strangers. The father, with a grand simplicity, either spoke of what interested himself, or maintained an unaffected silence. The son turned in his head for some topic that should be quite safe, that would spare him fresh evidences either of my lord's inherent grossness or of the innocence of his inhumanity; page 27 / 166

treading gingerly the ways of intercourse, like a lady gathering up her skirts in a by-path. If he made a mistake, and my lord began to abound in matter of offence, Archie drew himself up, his brow grew dark, his share of the talk expired; but my lord would faithfully and cheerfully continue to pour out the worst of himself before his silent and offended son.

"Well, it's a poor hert that never rejoices!" he would say, at the conclusion of such a nightmare interview. "But I must get to my plew-stilts." And he would seclude himself as usual in his back room, and Archie go forth into the night and the city quivering with animosity and scorn.

CHAPTER III - IN THE MATTER OF THE HANGING OF DUNCAN JOPP

IT chanced in the year 1813 that Archie strayed one day into the Justiciary Court. The macer made room for the son of the presiding judge. In the dock, the centre of men's eyes, there stood a whey-coloured, misbegotten caitiff, Duncan Jopp, on trial for his life. His story, as it was raked out before him in that public scene, was one of disgrace and vice and cowardice, the very nakedness of crime; and the creature heard and it seemed at times as though he understood - as if at times he forgot the horror of the place he stood in, and remembered the shame of what had brought him there. He kept his head bowed and his hands clutched upon the rail; his hair dropped in his eyes and at times he flung it back; and now he glanced about the audience in a sudden page 28 / 166

fellness of terror, and now looked in the face of his judge and gulped.

There was pinned about his throat a piece of dingy flannel; and this it was perhaps that turned the scale in Archie's mind between disgust and pity. The creature stood in a vanishing point; yet a little while, and he was still a man, and had eyes and apprehension; yet a little longer, and with a last sordid piece of pageantry, he would cease to be. And here, in the meantime, with a trait of human nature that caught at the beholder's breath, he was tending a sore throat.

Over against him, my Lord Hermiston occupied the bench in the red robes of criminal jurisdiction, his face framed in the white wig. Honest all through, he did not affect the virtue of impartiality; this was no case for refinement; there was a man to be hanged, he would have said, and he was hanging him. Nor was it possible to see his lordship, and acquit him of gusto in the task. It was plain he gloried in the exercise of his trained faculties, in the clear sight which pierced at once into the joint of fact, in the rude, unvarnished gibes with which he demolished every figment of defence. He took his ease and jested, unbending in that solemn place with some of the freedom of the tavern; and the rag of man with the flannel round his neck was hunted gallowsward with jeers.

Duncan had a mistress, scarce less forlorn and greatly older than himself, who came up, whimpering and curtseying, to add the weight of her betrayal. My lord gave her the oath in his most roaring voice, and added an intolerant warning.

"Mind what ye say now, Janet," said he. "I have an e'e upon ye, I'm ill to jest with."

Presently, after she was tremblingly embarked on her story, "And what made ye do this, ye auld runt?" the Court interposed. "Do ye mean to tell me ye was the panel's mistress?"

"If you please, ma loard," whined the female.

"Godsake! ye made a bonny couple," observed his lordship; and there was something so formidable and ferocious in his scorn that not even the galleries thought to laugh.

The summing up contained some jewels.

"These two peetiable creatures seem to have made up thegither, it's not for us to explain why." - "The panel, who (whatever else he may be) appears to be equally ill set-out in mind and boady." - "Neither the panel nor yet the old wife appears to have had so much common sense as even to tell a lie when it was necessary." And in the course of sentencing, my lord had this OBITER DICTUM: "I have been the means, under God, of haanging a great number, but never just such a disjaskit rascal as yourself." The words were strong in themselves; the light and heat and detonation of their delivery, and the savage pleasure of the speaker in his task, made them tingle in the ears.

page 30 / 166

When all was over, Archie came forth again into a changed world. Had there been the least redeeming greatness in the crime, any obscurity, any dubiety, perhaps he might have understood. But the culprit stood, with his sore throat, in the sweat of his mortal agony, without defence or excuse: a thing to cover up with blushes: a being so much sunk beneath the zones of sympathy that pity might seem harmless. And the judge had pursued him with a monstrous, relishing gaiety, horrible to be conceived, a trait for nightmares. It is one thing to spear a tiger, another to crush a toad; there are aesthetics even of the slaughter-house; and the loathsomeness of Duncan Jopp enveloped and infected the image of his judge.

Archie passed by his friends in the High Street with incoherent words and gestures. He saw Holyrood in a dream, remembrance of its romance awoke in him and faded; he had a vision of the old radiant stories, of Queen Mary and Prince Charlie, of the hooded stag, of the splendour and crime, the velvet and bright iron of the past; and dismissed them with a cry of pain. He lay and moaned in the Hunter's Bog, and the heavens were dark above him and the grass of the field an offence. "This is my father," he said. "I draw my life from him; the flesh upon my bones is his, the bread I am fed with is the wages of these horrors." He recalled his mother, and ground his forehead in the earth. He thought of flight, and where was he to flee to? of other lives, but was there any life worth living in this den of savage and jeering animals?

page 31 / 166

The interval before the execution was like a violent dream. He met his father; he would not look at him, he could not speak to him. It seemed there was no living creature but must have been swift to recognise that imminent animosity; but the hide of the Justice-Clerk remained impenetrable. Had my lord been talkative, the truce could never have subsisted; but he was by fortune in one of his humours of sour silence; and under the very guns of his broadside, Archie nursed the enthusiasm of rebellion. It seemed to him, from the top of his nineteen years'

experience, as if he were marked at birth to be the perpetrator of some signal action, to set back fallen Mercy, to overthrow the usurping devil that sat, horned and hoofed, on her throne. Seductive Jacobin figments, which he had often refuted at the Speculative, swam up in his mind and startled him as with voices: and he seemed to himself to walk accompanied by an almost tangible presence of new beliefs and duties.

On the named morning he was at the place of execution. He saw the fleering rabble, the flinching wretch produced. He looked on for a while at a certain parody of devotion, which seemed to strip the wretch of his last claim to manhood. Then followed the brutal instant of extinction, and the paltry dangling of the remains like a broken jumping-jack. He had been prepared for something terrible, not for this tragic meanness. He stood a moment silent, and then - "I denounce this God-defying murder," he shouted; and his father, if he must have disclaimed the sentiment, might have owned the stentorian voice with which it was uttered.

Frank Innes dragged him from the spot. The two handsome lads followed page 32 / 166 the same course of study and recreation, and felt a certain mutual attraction, founded mainly on good looks. It had never gone deep; Frank was by nature a thin, jeering creature, not truly susceptible whether of feeling or inspiring friendship; and the relation between the pair was altogether on the outside, a thing of common knowledge and the pleasantries that spring from a common acquaintance. The more credit to Frank that he was appalled by Archie's outburst, and at least conceived the design of keeping him in sight, and, if possible, in hand, for the day. But Archie, who had just defied - was it God or Satan? - would not listen to the word of a college companion.

"I will not go with you," he said. "I do not desire your company, sir; I would be alone."

"Here, Weir, man, don't be absurd," said Innes, keeping a tight hold upon his sleeve. "I will not let you go until I know what you mean to do with yourself; it's no use brandishing that staff." For indeed at that moment Archie had made a sudden - perhaps a warlike - movement.

"This has been the most insane affair; you know it has. You know very well that I'm playing the good Samaritan. All I wish is to keep you quiet."

"If quietness is what you wish, Mr. Innes," said Archie, "and you will promise to leave me entirely to myself, I will tell you so much, that I am going to walk in the country and admire the beauties of nature."

"Honour bright?" asked Frank.

"I am not in the habit of lying, Mr. Innes," retorted Archie. "I have the honour of wishing you good-day."

"You won't forget the Spec.?" asked Innes.

"The Spec.?" said Archie. "O no, I won't forget the Spec."

And the one young man carried his tortured spirit forth of the city and all the day long, by one road and another, in an endless pilgrimage of misery; while the other hastened smilingly to spread the news of Weir's access of insanity, and to drum up for that night a full attendance at the Speculative, where further eccentric developments might certainly be looked for. I doubt if Innes had the least belief in his prediction; I think it flowed rather from a wish to make the story as good and the scandal as great as possible; not from any ill-will to Archie - from the mere pleasure of beholding interested faces. But for all that his words were prophetic. Archie did not forget the Spec.; he put in an appearance there at the due time, and, before the evening was over, had dealt a memorable shock to his companions. It chanced he was the president of the night. He sat in the same room where the Society still meets - only the portraits were not there: the men who afterwards sat for them were then but beginning their career. The same lustre of many tapers shed its light over the meeting; the same chair, perhaps, page 34 / 166

supported him that so many of us have sat in since. At times he seemed to forget the business of the evening, but even in these periods he sat with a great air of energy and determination. At times he meddled bitterly, and launched with defiance those fines which are the precious and rarely used artillery of the president. He little thought, as he did so, how he resembled his father, but his friends remarked upon it, chuckling. So far, in his high place above his fellow-students, he seemed set beyond the possibility of any scandal; but his mind was made up - he was determined to fulfil the sphere of his offence. He signed to Innes (whom he had just fined, and who just impeached his ruling) to succeed him in the chair, stepped down from the platform, and took his place by the chimney-piece, the shine of many wax tapers from above illuminating his pale face, the glow of the great red fire relieving from behind his slim figure. He had to propose, as an amendment to the next subject in the case-book, "Whether capital punishment be consistent with God's will or man's policy?"

A breath of embarrassment, of something like alarm, passed round the room, so daring did these words appear upon the lips of Hermiston's only son. But the amendment was not seconded; the previous question was promptly moved and unanimously voted, and the momentary scandal smuggled by. Innes triumphed in the fulfilment of his prophecy. He and Archie were now become the heroes of the night; but whereas every one crowded about Innes, when the meeting broke up, but one of all his companions came to speak to Archie.

"Weir, man! That was an extraordinary raid of yours!" observed this page 35 / 166

courageous member, taking him confidentially by the arm as they went out.

"I don't think it a raid," said Archie grimly. "More like a war. I saw that poor brute hanged this morning, and my gorge rises at it yet."

"Hut-tut," returned his companion, and, dropping his arm like something hot, he sought the less tense society of others.

Archie found himself alone. The last of the faithful - or was it only the boldest of the curious? - had fled. He watched the black huddle of his fellow-students draw off down and up the street, in whispering or boisterous gangs. And the isolation of the moment weighed upon him like an omen and an emblem of his destiny in life. Bred up in unbroken fear himself, among trembling servants, and in a house which (at the least ruffle in the master's voice) shuddered into silence, he saw himself on the brink of the red valley of war, and measured the danger and length of it with awe. He made a detour in the glimmer and shadow of the streets, came into the back stable lane, and watched for a long while the light burn steady in the Judge's room. The longer he gazed upon that illuminated window-blind, the more blank became the picture of the man who sat behind it, endlessly turning over sheets of process, pausing to sip a glass of port, or rising and passing heavily about his book-lined walls to verify some reference. He could not combine the brutal judge and the industrious, dispassionate student; the connecting link escaped him; from such a dual nature, it was impossible he should page 36 / 166

predict behaviour; and he asked himself if he had done well to plunge into a business of which the end could not be foreseen? and presently after, with a sickening decline of confidence, if he had done loyally to strike his father? For he had struck him - defied him twice over and before a cloud of witnesses - struck him a public buffet before crowds.

Who had called him to judge his father in these precarious and high questions? The office was usurped. It might have become a stranger; in a son - there was no blinking it - in a son, it was disloyal. And now, between these two natures so antipathetic, so hateful to each other, there was depending an unpardonable affront: and the providence of

God alone might foresee the manner in which it would be resented by Lord Hermiston.

These misgivings tortured him all night and arose with him in the winter's morning; they followed him from class to class, they made him shrinkingly sensitive to every shade of manner in his companions, they sounded in his ears through the current voice of the professor; and he brought them home with him at night unabated and indeed increased. The cause of this increase lay in a chance encounter with the celebrated Dr.

Gregory. Archie stood looking vaguely in the lighted window of a book shop, trying to nerve himself for the approaching ordeal. My lord and he had met and parted in the morning as they had now done for long, with scarcely the ordinary civilities of life; and it was plain to the son that nothing had yet reached the father's ears. Indeed, when he recalled the awful countenance of my lord, a timid hope sprang up in him that perhaps there would be found no one bold enough to carry tales. If this were so, he asked himself, would he begin again? and he found no page 37 / 166

answer. It was at this moment that a hand was laid upon his arm, and a voice said in his ear, "My dear Mr. Archie, you had better come and see me."

He started, turned round, and found himself face to face with Dr.

Gregory. "And why should I come to see you?" he asked, with the defiance of the miserable.

"Because you are looking exceedingly ill," said the doctor, "and you very evidently want looking after, my young friend. Good folk are scarce, you know; and it is not every one that would be quite so much missed as yourself. It is not every one that Hermiston would miss."

And with a nod and a smile, the doctor passed on.

A moment after, Archie was in pursuit, and had in turn, but more roughly, seized him by the arm.

"What do you mean? what did you mean by saying that? What makes you think that Hermis - my father would have missed me?"

The doctor turned about and looked him all over with a clinical eye. A far more stupid man than Dr. Gregory might have guessed the truth; but ninety-nine out of a hundred, even if they had been equally inclined to kindness, would have blundered by some touch of charitable exaggeration.

page 38 / 166

The doctor was better inspired. He knew the father well; in that white face of intelligence and suffering, he divined something of the son; and he told, without apology or adornment, the plain truth.

"When you had the measles, Mr. Archibald, you had them gey and ill; and I thought you were going to slip between my fingers," he said. "Well, your father was anxious. How did I know it? says you. Simply because I am a trained observer. The sign that I saw him make, ten thousand would have missed; and perhaps - PERHAPS, I say, because he's a hard man to judge of - but perhaps he never made another. A strange thing to consider! It was this. One day I came to him: `Hermiston,' said I,

`there's a change.' He never said a word, just glowered at me (if ye'll pardon the phrase) like a wild beast. À change for the better,' said I. And I distinctly heard him take his breath."

The doctor left no opportunity for anti-climax; nodding his cocked hat (a piece of antiquity to which he clung) and repeating "Distinctly" with raised eye-brows, he took his departure, and left Archie speechless in the street.

The anecdote might be called infinitely little, and yet its meaning for Archie was immense. "I did not know the old man had so much blood in him." He had never dreamed this sire of his, this aboriginal antique, this adamantine Adam, had even so much of a heart as to be moved in the least degree for another - and that other himself, who had insulted him!

With the generosity of youth, Archie was instantly under arms upon the page 39 / 166

other side: had instantly created a new image of Lord Hermiston, that of a man who was all iron without and all sensibility within. The mind of the vile jester, the tongue that had pursued Duncan Jopp with unmanly insults, the unbeloved countenance that he had known and feared for so long, were all forgotten; and he hastened home, impatient to confess his misdeeds, impatient to throw himself on the mercy of this imaginary character.

He was not to be long without a rude awakening. It was in the gloaming when he drew near the door-step of the lighted house, and was aware of the figure of his father approaching from the opposite side. Little daylight lingered; but on the door being opened, the strong yellow shine of the lamp gushed out upon the landing and shone full on Archie, as he stood, in the old-fashioned observance of respect, to yield precedence.

The judge came without haste, stepping stately and firm; his chin raised, his face (as he entered the lamplight) strongly illumined, his mouth set hard. There was never a wink of change in his expression; without looking to the right or left, he mounted the stair, passed close to Archie, and entered the house. Instinctively, the boy, upon his first coming, had made a movement to meet him; instinctively he recoiled against the railing, as the old man swept by him in a pomp of indignation. Words were needless; he knew all - perhaps more than all -

and the hour of judgment was at hand.

It is possible that, in this sudden revulsion of hope, and before these symptoms of impending danger, Archie might have fled. But not even that was left to him. My lord, after hanging up his cloak and hat, turned page 40 / 166

round in the lighted entry, and made him an imperative and silent gesture with his thumb, and with the strange instinct of obedience, Archie followed him into the house.

All dinner-time there reigned over the Judge's table a palpable silence, and as soon as the solids were despatched he rose to his feet.

"M'Killup, tak' the wine into my room," said he; and then to his son:

"Archie, you and me has to have a talk."

It was at this sickening moment that Archie's courage, for the first and last time, entirely deserted him. "I have an appointment," said he.

"It'll have to be broken, then," said Hermiston, and led the way into his study.

The lamp was shaded, the fire trimmed to a nicety, the table covered deep with orderly documents, the backs of law books made a frame upon all sides that was only broken by the window and the doors.

For a moment Hermiston warmed his hands at the fire, presenting his back to Archie; then suddenly disclosed on him the terrors of the Hanging Face.

"What's this I hear of ye?" he asked.

There was no answer possible to Archie.

"I'll have to tell ye, then," pursued Hermiston. "It seems ye've been skirting against the father that begot ye, and one of his Maijesty's Judges in this land; and that in the public street, and while an order of the Court was being executit. Forbye which, it would appear that ye've been airing your opeenions in a Coallege Debatin' Society"; he paused a moment: and then, with extraordinary bitterness, added: "Ye damned eediot."

"I had meant to tell you," stammered Archie. "I see you are well informed."

"Muckle obleeged to ye," said his lordship, and took his usual seat.

"And so you disapprove of Caapital Punishment?" he added.

"I am sorry, sir, I do," said Archie.

"I am sorry, too," said his lordship. "And now, if you please, we shall approach this business with a little more parteecularity. I hear that at the hanging of Duncan Jopp - and, man! ye had a fine client there -

in the middle of all the riff-raff of the ceety, ye thought fit to cry out, `This is a damned murder, and my gorge rises at the man that page 42 / 166

haangit him.' "

"No, sir, these were not my words," cried Archie.

"What were yer words, then?" asked the Judge.

"I believe I said, Ì denounce it as a murder!'" said the son. "I beg your pardon - a God-defying murder. I have no wish to conceal the truth," he added, and looked his father for a moment in the face.

"God, it would only need that of it next!" cried Hermiston. "There was nothing about your gorge rising, then?"

"That was afterwards, my lord, as I was leaving the Speculative. I said I had been to see the miserable creature hanged, and my gorge rose at it."

"Did ye, though?" said Hermiston. "And I suppose ye knew who haangit him?"

"I was present at the trial, I ought to tell you that, I ought to explain. I ask your pardon beforehand for any expression that may seem undutiful. The position in which I stand is wretched," said the unhappy hero, now fairly face to face with the business he had chosen. "I have page 43 / 166

been reading some of your cases. I was present while Jopp was tried.

It was a hideous business. Father, it was a hideous thing! Grant he was vile, why should you hunt him with a vileness equal to his own? It was done with glee - that is the word - you did it with glee; and I looked on, God help me! with horror."

"You're a young gentleman that doesna approve of Caapital Punishment,"

said Hermiston. "Weel, I'm an auld man that does. I was glad to get Jopp haangit, and what for would I pretend I wasna? You're all for honesty, it seems; you couldn't even steik your mouth on the public street. What for should I steik mines upon the bench, the King's officer, bearing the sword, a dreid to evil-doers, as I was from the beginning, and as I will be to the end! Mair than enough of it!

Heedious! I never gave twa thoughts to heediousness, I have no call to be bonny. I'm a man that gets through with my day's business, and let that suffice."

The ring of sarcasm had died out of his voice as he went on; the plain words became invested with some of the dignity of the Justice-seat.

"It would be telling you if you could say as much," the speaker resumed.

"But ye cannot. Ye've been reading some of my cases, ye say. But it was not for the law in them, it was to spy out your faither's nakedness, a fine employment in a son. You're splairging; you're running at lairge in life like a wild nowt. It's impossible you should think any longer of coming to the Bar. You're not fit for it; no splairger is. And another thing: son of mines or no son of mines, you have flung fylement in public on one of the Senators of the Coallege of Justice, and I would make it my business to see that ye were never admitted there yourself.

There is a kind of a decency to be observit. Then comes the next of it

- what am I to do with ye next? Ye'll have to find some kind of a trade, for I'll never support ye in idleset. What do ye fancy ye'll be fit for? The pulpit? Na, they could never get diveenity into that bloackhead. Him that the law of man whammles is no likely to do muckle better by the law of God. What would ye make of hell? Wouldna your gorge rise at that? Na, there's no room for splairgers under the fower quarters of John Calvin. What else is there? Speak up. Have ye got nothing of your own?"

"Father, let me go to the Peninsula," said Archie. "That's all I'm fit for - to fight."

"All? quo' he!" returned the Judge. "And it would be enough too, if I thought it. But I'll never trust ye so near the French, you that's so Frenchi-feed."

"You do me injustice there, sir," said Archie. "I am loyal; I will not boast; but any interest I may have ever felt in the French - "

"Have ye been so loyal to me?" interrupted his father.

There came no reply.

"I think not," continued Hermiston. "And I would send no man to be a servant to the King, God bless him! that has proved such a shauchling son to his own faither. You can splairge here on Edinburgh street, and where's the hairm? It doesna play buff on me! And if there were twenty thousand eediots like yourself, sorrow a Duncan Jopp would hang the fewer. But there's no splairging possible in a camp; and if ye were to go to it, you would find out for yourself whether Lord Well'n'ton approves of caapital punishment or not. You a sodger!" he cried, with a sudden burst of scorn. "Ye auld wife, the sodgers would bray at ye like cuddies!"

As at the drawing of a curtain, Archie was aware of some illogicality in his position, and stood abashed. He had a strong impression, besides, of the essential valour of the old gentleman before him, how conveyed it would be hard to say.

"Well, have ye no other proposeetion?" said my lord again.

"You have taken this so calmly, sir, that I cannot but stand ashamed,"

began Archie.

"I'm nearer voamiting, though, than you would fancy," said my lord.

The blood rose to Archie's brow.

"I beg your pardon, I should have said that you had accepted my affront.

. . . I admit it was an affront; I did not think to apologise, but I do, I ask your pardon; it will not be so again, I pass you my word of honour. . . . I should have said that I admired your magnanimity with -

this - offender," Archie concluded with a gulp.

"I have no other son, ye see," said Hermiston. "A bonny one I have gotten! But I must just do the best I can wi' him, and what am I to do?

If ye had been younger, I would have wheepit ye for this rideeculous exhibeetion. The way it is, I have just to grin and bear. But one thing is to be clearly understood. As a faither, I must grin and bear it; but if I had been the Lord Advocate instead of the Lord Justice-Clerk, son or no son, Mr. Erchibald Weir would have been in a jyle the night."

Archie was now dominated. Lord Hermiston was coarse and cruel; and yet the son was aware of a bloomless nobility, an ungracious abnegation of the man's self in the man's office. At every word, this sense of the greatness of Lord Hermiston's spirit struck more home; and along with it that of his own impotence, who had struck - and perhaps basely struck -

at his own father, and not reached so far as to have even nettled him.

"I place myself in your hands without reserve," he said.

page 47 / 166

"That's the first sensible word I've had of ye the night," said Hermiston. "I can tell ye, that would have been the end of it, the one way or the other; but it's better ye should come there yourself, than what I would have had to hirstle ye. Weel, by my way of it - and my way is the best - there's just the one thing it's possible that ye might be with decency, and that's a laird. Ye'll be out of hairm's way at the least of it. If ye have to rowt, ye can rowt amang the kye; and the maist feck of the caapital punishmeiit ye're like to come across'll be guddling trouts. Now, I'm for no idle lairdies; every man has to work, if it's only at peddling ballants; to work, or to be wheeped, or to be haangit. If I set ye down at Hermiston I'll have to see you work that place the way it has never been workit yet; ye must ken about the sheep like a herd; ye must be my grieve there, and I'll see that I gain by ye.

Is that understood?"

"I will do my best," said Archie.

"Well, then, I'll send Kirstie word the morn, and ye can go yourself the day after," said Hermiston. "And just try to be less of an eediot!" he concluded with a freezing smile, and turned immediately to the papers on his desk.

CHAPTER IV - OPINIONS OF THE BENCH

LATE the same night, after a disordered walk, Archie was admitted into Lord Glenalmond's dining-room, where he sat with a book upon his knee, page 48 / 166

beside three frugal coals of fire. In his robes upon the bench, Glenalmond had a certain air of burliness: plucked of these, it was a may-pole of a man that rose unsteadily from his chair to give his visitor welcome. Archie had suffered much in the last days, he had suffered again that evening; his face was white and drawn, his eyes wild and dark. But Lord Glenalmond greeted him without the least mark of surprise or curiosity.

"Come in, come in," said he. "Come in and take a seat. Carstairs" (to his servant), "make up the fire, and then you can bring a bit of supper," and again to Archie, with a very trivial accent: "I was half expecting you," he added.

"No supper," said Archie. "It is impossible that I should eat."

"Not impossible," said the tall old man, laying his hand upon his shoulder, "and, if you will believe me, necessary."

"You know what brings me?" said Archie, as soon as the servant had left the room.

"I have a guess, I have a guess," replied Glenalmond. "We will talk of it presently - when Carstairs has come and gone, and you have had a piece of my good Cheddar cheese and a pull at the porter tankard: not before."

page 49 / 166

"It is impossible I should eat" repeated Archie.

"Tut, tut!" said Lord Glenalmond. "You have eaten nothing to-day, and I venture to add, nothing yesterday. There is no case that may not be made worse; this may be a very disagreeable business, but if you were to fall sick and die, it would be still more so, and for all concerned -

for all concerned."

"I see you must know all," said Archie. "Where did you hear it?"

"In the mart of scandal, in the Parliament House," said Glenalmond. "It runs riot below among the bar and the public, but it sifts up to us upon the bench, and rumour has some of her voices even in the divisions."

Carstairs returned at this moment, and rapidly laid out a little supper; during which Lord Glenalmond spoke at large and a little vaguely on indifferent subjects, so that it might be rather said of him that he made a cheerful noise, than that he contributed to human conversation; and Archie sat upon the other side, not heeding him, brooding over his wrongs and errors.

But so soon as the servant was gone, he broke forth again at once. "Who told my father? Who dared to tell him? Could it have been you?"

"No, it was not me," said the Judge; "although - to be quite frank with you, and after I had seen and warned you - it might have been me - I believe it was Glenkindie."

"That shrimp!" cried Archie.

"As you say, that shrimp," returned my lord; "although really it is scarce a fitting mode of expression for one of the senators of the College of Justice. We were hearing the parties in a long, crucial case, before the fifteen; Creech was moving at some length for an infeftment; when I saw Glenkindie lean forward to Hermiston with his hand over his mouth and make him a secret communication. No one could have guessed its nature from your father: from Glenkindie, yes, his malice sparked out of him a little grossly. But your father, no. A man of granite. The next moment he pounced upon Creech. `Mr. Creech,' says he, `I'll take a look of that sasine,' and for thirty minutes after,"

said Glenalmond, with a smile, "Messrs. Creech and Co. were fighting a pretty up-hill battle, which resulted, I need hardly add, in their total rout. The case was dismissed. No,

I doubt if ever I heard Hermiston better inspired. He was literally rejoicing IN APICIBUS JURIS."

Archie was able to endure no longer. He thrust his plate away and interrupted the deliberate and insignificant stream of talk. "Here," he said, "I have made a fool of myself, if I have not made something worse.

Do you judge between us - judge between a father and a son. I can speak page 51 / 166

to you; it is not like ... I will tell you what I feel and what I mean to do; and you shall be the judge," he repeated.

"I decline jurisdiction," said Glenalmond, with extreme seriousness.

"But, my dear boy, if it will do you any good to talk, and if it will interest you at all to hear what I may choose to say when I have heard you, I am quite at your command. Let an old man say it, for once, and not need to blush: I love you like a son."

There came a sudden sharp sound in Archie's throat. "Ay," he cried,

"and there it is! Love! Like a son! And how do you think I love my father?"

"Quietly, quietly," says my lord.

"I will be very quiet," replied Archie. "And I will be baldly frank. I do not love my father; I wonder sometimes if I do not hate him. There's my shame; perhaps my sin; at least, and in the sight of God, not my fault. How was I to love him? He has never spoken to me, never smiled upon me; I do not think he ever touched me. You know the way he talks?

You do not talk so, yet you can sit and hear him without shuddering, and I cannot. My soul is sick when he begins with it; I could smite him in the mouth. And all that's nothing. I was at the trial of this Jopp.

You were not there, but you must have heard him often; the man's notorious for it, for being - look at my position! he's my father and this is how I have to speak of him - notorious for being a brute and page 52 / 166

cruel and a coward. Lord Glenalmond, I give you my word, when I came out of that Court, I longed to die - the shame of it was beyond my strength: but I - I -" he rose from his seat and began to pace the room in a disorder. "Well, who am I? A boy, who have never been tried, have never done anything except this twopenny impotent folly with my father.

But I tell you, my lord, and I know myself, I am at least that kind of a man - or that kind of a boy, if you prefer it - that I could die in torments rather than that any one should suffer as that scoundrel suffered. Well, and what have I done? I see it now. I have made a fool of myself, as I said in the beginning; and I have gone back, and asked my father's pardon, and placed myself wholly in his hands - and he has sent me to Hermiston," with a wretched smile, "for life, I suppose -

and what can I say? he strikes me as having done quite right, and let me off better than I had deserved."

"My poor, dear boy!" observed Glenalmond. "My poor dear and, if you will allow me to say so, very foolish boy! You are only discovering where you are; to one of your temperament, or of mine, a painful discovery. The world was not made for us; it was made for ten hundred millions of men, all different from each other and from us; there's no royal road there, we just have to sclamber and tumble. Don't think that I am at all disposed to be surprised; don't suppose that I ever think of blaming you; indeed I rather admire! But there fall to be offered one or two observations on the case which occur to me and which (if you will listen to them dispassionately) may be the means of inducing you to view the matter more calmly. First of all, I cannot acquit you of a good deal of what is called intolerance. You seem to have been very much page 53 / 166

offended because your father talks a little sculduddery after dinner, which it is perfectly licit for him to do, and which (although I am not very fond of it myself) appears to be entirely an affair of taste. Your father, I scarcely like to remind you, since it is so trite a commonplace, is older than yourself. At least, he is MAJOR and SUI JURIS, and may please himself in the matter of his conversation. And, do you know, I wonder if he might not have as good an answer against you and me? We say we sometimes find him COARSE, but I suspect he might retort that he finds us always dull. Perhaps a relevant exception."

He beamed on Archie, but no smile could be elicited.

"And now," proceeded the Judge, "for Àrchibald on Capital Punishment.'

This is a very plausible academic opinion; of course I do not and I cannot hold it; but that's not to say that many able and excellent persons have not done so in the past. Possibly, in the past also, I may have a little dipped myself in the same heresy. My third client, or possibly my fourth, was the means of a return in my opinions. I never saw the man I more believed in; I would have put my hand in the fire, I would have gone to the cross for him; and when it came to trial he was gradually pictured before me, by undeniable probation, in the light of so gross, so cold-blooded, and so black-hearted a villain, that I had a mind to have cast my brief upon the table. I was then boiling against the man with even a more tropical temperature than I had been boiling for him. But I said to myself: `No, you have taken up his case; and because you have changed your mind it must not be suffered to let drop.

All that rich tide of eloquence that you prepared last night with so page 54 / 166

much enthusiasm is out of place, and yet you must not desert him, you must say something.' So I said something, and I got him off. It made my reputation. But an experience of that kind is formative. A man must not bring his passions to the bar - or to the bench," he added.

The story had slightly rekindled Archie's interest. "I could never deny," he began - "I mean I can conceive that some men would be better dead. But who are we to know all the springs of God's unfortunate creatures? Who are we to trust ourselves where it seems that God Himself must think twice before He treads, and to do it with delight?

Yes, with delight. TIGRIS UT ASPERA."

"Perhaps not a pleasant spectacle," said Glenalmond. "And yet, do you know, I think somehow a great one."

"I've had a long talk with him to-night," said Archie.

"I was supposing so," said Glenalmond.

"And he struck me - I cannot deny that he struck me as something very big," pursued the son. "Yes, he is big. He never spoke about himself; only about me. I suppose I admired him. The dreadful part - "

"Suppose we did not talk about that," interrupted Glenalmond. "You know it very well, it cannot in any way help that you should brood upon it, page 55 / 166

and I sometimes wonder whether you and I - who are a pair of sentimentalists - are quite good judges of plain men."

"How do you mean?" asked Archie.

"FAIR judges, mean," replied Glenalmond. "Can we be just to them? Do we not ask too much? There was a word of yours just now that impressed me a little when you asked me who we were to know all the springs of God's unfortunate creatures. You applied that, as I understood, to capital cases only. But does it - I ask myself - does it not apply all through? Is it any less difficult to judge of a good man or of a half-good man, than of the worst criminal at the bar? And may not each have relevant excuses?"

"Ah, but we do not talk of punishing the good," cried Archie.

"No, we do not talk of it," said Glenalmond. "But I think we do it. Your father, for instance."

"You think I have punished him?" cried Archie.

Lord Glenalmond bowed his head.

"I think I have," said Archie. "And the worst is, I think he feels it!

How much, who can tell, with such a being? But I think he does."

"And I am sure of it," said Glenalmond.

"Has he spoken to you, then?" cried Archie.

"O no," replied the judge.

"I tell you honestly," said Archie, "I want to make it up to him. I will go, I have already pledged myself to go to Hermiston. That was to him. And now I pledge myself to you, in the sight of God, that I will close my mouth on capital punishment and all other subjects where our views may clash, for - how long shall I say? when shall I have sense enough? - ten years. Is that well?"

"It is well," said my lord.

"As far as it goes," said Archie. "It is enough as regards myself, it is to lay down enough of my conceit. But as regards him, whom I have publicly insulted? What am I to do to him? How do you pay attentions to a - an Alp like that?"

"Only in one way," replied Glenalmond. "Only by obedience, punctual, prompt, and scrupulous."

"And I promise that he shall have it," answered Archie. "I offer you my hand in pledge of it."

"And I take your hand as a solemnity," replied the judge. "God bless you, my dear, and enable you to keep your promise. God guide you in the true way, and spare your days, and preserve to you your honest heart."

At that, he kissed the young man upon the forehead in a gracious, distant, antiquated way; and instantly launched, with a marked change of voice, into another subject. "And now, let us replenish the tankard; and I believe if you will try my Cheddar again, you would find you had a better appetite. The Court has spoken, and the case is dismissed."

"No, there is one thing I must say," cried Archie. "I must say it in justice to himself. I know - I believe faithfully, slavishly, after our talk - he will never ask me anything unjust. I am proud to feel it, that we have that much in common, I am proud to say it to you."

The Judge, with shining eyes, raised his tankard. "And I think perhaps that we might permit ourselves a toast," said he. "I should like to propose the health of a man very different from me and very much my superior - a man from whom I have often differed, who has often (in the trivial expression) rubbed me the wrong way, but whom I have never ceased to respect and, I may add, to be not a little afraid of. Shall I give you his name?"

"The Lord Justice-Clerk, Lord Hermiston," said Archie, almost with gaiety; and the pair drank the toast deeply.

It was not precisely easy to re-establish, after these emotional passages, the natural flow of conversation. But the Judge eked out what was wanting with kind looks, produced his snuff-box (which was very rarely seen) to fill in a pause, and at last, despairing of any further social success, was upon the point of getting down a book to read a favourite passage, when there came a rather startling summons at the front door, and Carstairs ushered in my Lord Glenkindie, hot from a midnight supper. I am not aware that Glenkindie was ever a beautiful object, being short, and gross-bodied, and with an expression of sensuality comparable to a bear's. At that moment, coming in hissing from many potations, with a flushed countenance and blurred eyes, he was strikingly contrasted with the tall, pale, kingly figure of Glenalmond.

A rush of confused thought came over Archie - of shame that this was one of his father's elect friends; of pride, that at the least of it Hermiston could carry his liquor; and last of all, of rage, that he should have here under his eyes the man that had betrayed him. And then that too passed away; and he sat quiet, biding his opportunity.

The tipsy senator plunged at once into an explanation with Glenalmond.

There was a point reserved yesterday, he had been able to make neither head nor tail of it, and seeing lights in the house, he had just dropped in for a glass of porter - and at this point he became aware of the third person. Archie saw the cod's mouth and the blunt lips of page 59 / 166

Glenkindie gape at him for a moment, and the recognition twinkle in his eyes.

"Who's this?" said he. "What? is this possibly you, Don Quickshot? And how are ye? And how's your father? And what's all this we hear of you?

It seems you're a most extraordinary leveller, by all tales. No king, no parliaments, and your gorge rises at the macers, worthy men! Hoot, toot! Dear, dear me! Your father's son too! Most rideeculous!"

Archie was on his feet, flushing a little at the reappearance of his unhappy figure of speech, but perfectly self-possessed. "My lord - and you, Lord Glenalmond, my dear friend," he began, "this is a happy chance for me, that I can make my confession and offer my apologies to two of you at once."

"Ah, but I don't know about that. Confession? It'll be judeecial, my young friend," cried the jocular Glenkindie. "And I'm afraid to listen to ye. Think if ye were to make me a coanvert!"

"If you would allow me, my lord," returned Archie, "what I have to say is very serious to me; and be pleased to be humorous after I am gone!"

"Remember, I'll hear nothing against the macers!" put in the incorrigible Glenkindie.

page 60 / 166

But Archie continued as though he had not spoken. "I have played, both yesterday and to-day, a part for which I can only offer the excuse of youth. I was so unwise as to go to an execution; it seems I made a scene at the gallows; not content with which, I spoke the same night in a college society against capital punishment. This is the extent of what I have done, and in case you hear more alleged against me, I protest my innocence. I have expressed my regret already to my father, who is so good as to pass my conduct over - in a degree, and upon the condition that I am to leave my law studies." . . .

CHAPTER V - WINTER ON THE MOORS

I. AT HERMISTON

THE road to Hermiston runs for a great part of the way up the valley of a stream, a favourite with anglers and with midges, full of falls and pools, and shaded by willows and natural woods of birch. Here and there, but at great distances, a byway branches off, and a gaunt farmhouse may be descried above in a fold of the hill; but the more part of the time, the road would be quite empty of passage and the hills of habitation. Hermiston parish is one of the least populous in Scotland; and, by the time you came that length, you would scarce be surprised at the inimitable smallness of the kirk, a dwarfish, ancient place seated for fifty, and standing in a green by the burn-side among two-score gravestones. The manse close by, although no more than a cottage, is surrounded by the brightness of a flower-garden and the straw roofs of page 61 / 166

bees; and the whole colony, kirk and manse, garden and graveyard, finds harbourage in a grove of rowans, and is all the year round in a great silence broken only by the drone of the bees, the tinkle of the burn, and the bell on Sundays. A mile beyond the kirk the road leaves the valley by a precipitous ascent, and brings you a little after to the place of Hermiston, where it comes to an end in the back-yard before the coach-house. All beyond and about is the great field, of the hills; the plover, the curlew, and the lark cry there; the wind blows as it blows in a ship's rigging, hard and cold and pure; and the hill-tops huddle one behind another like a herd of cattle into the sunset.

The house was sixty years old, unsightly, comfortable; a farmyard and a kitchen-garden on the left, with a fruit wall where little hard green pears came to their maturity about the end of October.

The policy (as who should say the park) was of some extent, but very ill reclaimed; heather and moorfowl had crossed the boundary wall and spread and roosted within; and it would have tasked a landscape gardener to say where policy ended and unpolicied nature began. My lord had been led by the influence of Mr. Sheriff Scott into a considerable design of planting; many acres were accordingly set out with fir, and the little feathery besoms gave a false scale and lent a strange air of a toy-shop to the moors. A great, rooty sweetness of bogs was in the air, and at all seasons an infinite melancholy piping of hill birds. Standing so high and with so little shelter, it was a cold, exposed house, splashed by showers, drenched by continuous rains that made the gutters to spout, beaten upon and buffeted by all the winds of heaven; and the prospect page 62 / 166

would be often black with tempest, and often white with the snows of winter. But the house was wind and weather proof, the hearths were kept bright, and the rooms pleasant with live fires of peat; and Archie might sit of an evening and hear the squalls bugle on the moorland, and watch the fire prosper in the earthy fuel, and the smoke winding up the chimney, and drink deep of the pleasures of shelter.

Solitary as the place was, Archie did not want neighbours. Every night, if he chose, he might go down to the manse and share a "brewst" of toddy with the minister - a hare-brained ancient gentleman, long and light and still active, though his knees were loosened with age, and his voice broke continually in childish trebles - and his lady wife, a heavy, comely dame, without a word to say for herself beyond good-even and good-day. Harum-scarum, clodpole young lairds of the neighbourhood paid him the compliment of a visit. Young Hay of Romanes rode down to call, on his crop-eared pony; young Pringle of Drumanno came up on his bony grey. Hay remained on the hospitable field, and must be carried to bed; Pringle got somehow to his saddle about 3 A.M., and (as Archie stood with the lamp on the upper doorstep) lurched, uttered a senseless view-holloa, and vanished out of the small circle of illumination like a wraith. Yet a minute or two longer the clatter of his break-neck flight was audible, then it was cut off by the intervening steepness of the hill; and again, a great while after, the renewed beating of phantom horse-hoofs, far in the valley of the Hermiston, showed that the horse at least, if not his rider, was still on the homeward way.

There was a Tuesday club at the "Cross-keys" in Crossmichael, where the page 63 / 166

young bloods of the country-side congregated and drank deep on a percentage of the expense, so that he was left gainer who should have drunk the most. Archie had no great mind to this diversion, but he took it like a duty laid upon him, went with a decent regularity, did his manfullest with the liquor, held up his head in the local jests, and got home again and was able to put up his horse, to the admiration of Kirstie and the lass that helped her. He dined at Driffel, supped at Windielaws. He went to the new year's ball at Huntsfield and was made welcome, and thereafter rode to hounds with my Lord Muirfell, upon whose name, as that of a legitimate Lord of Parliament, in a work so full of Lords of Session, my pen should pause reverently. Yet the same fate attended him here as in Edinburgh. The habit of solitude tends to perpetuate itself, and an austerity of which he was quite unconscious, and a pride which seemed arrogance, and perhaps was chiefly shyness, discouraged and offended his new companions. Hay did not return more than twice, Pringle never at all, and there came a time when Archie even desisted from the Tuesday Club, and became in all things - what he had had the name of almost from the first - the Recluse of Hermiston.

High-nosed Miss Pringle of Drumanno and high-stepping Miss Marshall of the Mains were understood to have had a difference of opinion about him the day after the ball - he was none the wiser, he could not suppose himself to be remarked by these entrancing ladies. At the ball itself my Lord Muirfell's daughter, the Lady Flora, spoke to him twice, and the second time with a touch of appeal, so that her colour rose and her voice trembled a little in his ear, like a passing grace in music. He stepped back with a heart on fire, coldly and not ungracefully excused himself, and a little after watched her dancing with young Drumanno of the empty laugh, and was harrowed at the sight, and raged to himself page 64 / 166

that this was a world in which it was given to Drumanno to please, and to himself only to stand aside and envy. He seemed excluded, as of right, from the favour of such society - seemed to extinguish mirth wherever he came, and was quick to feel the wound, and desist, and retire into solitude. If he had but understood the figure he presented, and the impression he made on these bright eyes and tender hearts; if he had but guessed that the Recluse of Hermiston, young, graceful, well spoken, but always cold, stirred the maidens of the county with the charm of Byronism when Byronism was new, it may be questioned whether his destiny might not even yet have been modified. It may be questioned, and I think it should be doubted. It was in his horoscope to be parsimonious of pain to himself, or of the chance of pain, even to the avoidance of any opportunity of pleasure; to have a Roman sense of duty, an instinctive aristocracy of manners and taste; to be the son of Adam Weir and Jean Rutherford.

2. KIRSTIE

Kirstie was now over fifty, and might have sat to a sculptor. Long of limb, and still light of foot, deep-breasted, robust-loined, her golden hair not yet mingled with any trace of silver, the years had but caressed and embellished her. By the lines of a rich and vigorous maternity, she seemed destined to be the bride of heroes and the mother of their children; and behold, by the iniquity of fate, she had passed through her youth alone, and drew near to the confines of age, a childless woman. The tender ambitions that she had received at birth had been, by time and disappointment, diverted into a certain barren page 65 / 166

zeal of industry and fury of interference. She carried her thwarted ardours into housework, she washed floors with her empty heart. If she could not win the love of one with love, she must dominate all by her temper. Hasty, wordy, and wrathful, she had a drawn quarrel with most of her neighbours, and with the others not much more than armed neutrality. The grieve's wife had been "sneisty"; the sister of the gardener who kept house for him had shown herself "upsitten"; and she wrote to Lord Hermiston about once a year demanding the discharge of the offenders, and justifying the demand by much wealth of detail. For it must not be supposed that the quarrel rested with the wife and did not take in the husband also - or with the gardener's sister, and did not speedily include the gardener himself. As the upshot of all this petty quarrelling and intemperate speech, she was practically excluded (like a lightkeeper on his tower) from the comforts of human association; except with her own indoor drudge, who, being but a lassie and entirely at her mercy, must submit to the shifty weather of "the mistress's" moods without complaint, and be willing to take buffets or caresses according to the temper of the hour. To Kirstie, thus situate and in the Indian summer of her heart, which was slow to submit to age, the gods sent this equivocal good thing of Archie's presence. She had known him in the cradle and paddled him when he misbehaved; and yet, as she had not so much as set eyes on him since he was eleven and had his last serious illness, the tall, slender, refined, and rather melancholy young gentleman of twenty came upon her with the shock of a new acquaintance.

He was "Young Hermiston," "the laird himsel' ": he had an air of distinctive superiority, a cold straight glance of his black eyes, that abashed the woman's tantrums in the beginning, and therefore the possibility of any quarrel was excluded. He was new, and therefore page 66 / 166

immediately aroused her curiosity; he was reticent, and kept it awake.

And lastly he was dark and she fair, and he was male and she female, the everlasting fountains of interest.

Her feeling partook of the loyalty of a clanswoman, the hero-worship of a maiden aunt, and the idolatry due to a god. No matter what he had asked of her, ridiculous or tragic, she would have done it and joyed to do it. Her passion, for it was nothing less, entirely filled her. It was a rich physical pleasure to make his bed or light his lamp for him when he was absent, to pull off his wet boots or wait on him at dinner when he returned. A young man who should have so doted on the idea, moral and physical, of any woman, might be properly described as being in love, head and heels, and would have behaved himself accordingly.

But Kirstie - though her heart leaped at his coming footsteps - though, when he patted her shoulder, her face brightened for the day - had not a hope or thought beyond the present moment and its perpetuation to the end of time. Till the end of time she would have had nothing altered, but still continue delightedly to serve her idol, and be repaid (say twice in the month) with a clap on the shoulder.

I have said her heart leaped - it is the accepted phrase. But rather, when she was alone in any chamber of the house, and heard his foot passing on the corridors, something in her bosom rose slowly until her breath was suspended, and as slowly fell again with a deep sigh, when the steps had passed and she was disappointed of her eyes' desire. This perpetual hunger and thirst of his presence kept her all day on the alert. When he went forth at morning, she would stand and follow him page 67 / 166

with admiring looks. As it grew late and drew to the time of his return, she would steal forth to a corner of the policy wall and be seen standing there sometimes by the hour together, gazing with shaded eyes, waiting the exquisite and barren pleasure of his view a mile off on the mountains.

When at night she had trimmed and gathered the fire, turned down his bed, and laid out his night-gear - when there was no more to be done for the king's pleasure, but to remember him fervently in her usually very tepid prayers, and go to bed brooding upon his perfections, his future career, and what she should give him the next day for dinner - there still remained before her one more opportunity; she was still to take in the tray and say good-night. Sometimes Archie would glance up from his book with a preoccupied nod and a perfunctory salutation which was in truth a dismissal; sometimes - and by degrees more often - the volume would be laid aside, he would meet her coming with a look of relief; and the conversation would be engaged, last out the supper, and be prolonged till the small hours by the waning fire. It was no wonder that Archie was fond of company after his solitary days; and Kirstie, upon her side, exerted all the arts of her vigorous nature to ensnare his attention.

She would keep back some piece of news during dinner to be fired off with the entrance of the supper tray, and form as it were the LEVER DE

RIDEAU of the evening's entertainment. Once he had heard her tongue wag, she made sure of the result. From one subject to another she moved by insidious transitions, fearing the least silence, fearing almost to give him time for an answer lest it should slip into a hint of separation. Like so many people of her class, she was a brave narrator; her place was on the hearth-rug and she made it a rostrum, mimeing her stories as she told them, fitting them with vital detail, spinning them out with endless "quo' he's" and "quo' she's," her voice sinking into a page 68 / 166

whisper over the supernatural or the horrific; until she would suddenly spring up in affected surprise, and pointing to the clock, "Mercy, Mr.

Archie!" she would say, "whatten a time o' night is this of it! God forgive me for a daft wife!" So it befell, by good management, that she was not only the first to begin these nocturnal conversations, but invariably the first to break them off; so she managed to retire and not to be dismissed.

3. A BORDER FAMILY

Such an unequal intimacy has never been uncommon in Scotland, where the clan spirit survives; where the servant tends to spend her life in the same service, a helpmeet at first, then a tyrant, and at last a pensioner; where, besides, she is not necessarily destitute of the pride of birth, but is, perhaps, like Kirstie, a connection of her master's, and at least knows the legend of her own family, and may count kinship with some illustrious dead. For that is the mark of the Scot of all classes: that he stands in an attitude towards the past unthinkable to Englishmen, and remembers and cherishes the memory of his forebears, good or bad; and there burns alive in him a sense of identity with the dead even to the twentieth generation. No more characteristic instance could be found than in the family of Kirstie Elliott. They were all, and Kirstie the first of all, ready and eager to pour forth the particulars of their genealogy, embellished with every detail that memory had handed down or fancy fabricated; and, behold! from every ramification of that tree there dangled a halter. The Elliotts themselves have had a chequered history; but these Elliotts deduced, page 69 / 166

besides, from three of the most unfortunate of the border clans - the Nicksons, the Ellwalds, and the Crozers. One ancestor after another might be seen appearing a moment out of the rain and the hill mist upon his furtive business, speeding home, perhaps, with a paltry booty of lame horses and lean kine, or squealing and dealing death in some moorland feud of the ferrets and the wild cats. One after another closed his obscure adventures in mid-air, triced up to the arm of the royal gibbet or the Baron's dule-tree. For the rusty blunderbuss of Scots criminal justice, which usually hurt nobody but jurymen, became a weapon of precision for the Nicksons, the Ellwalds, and the Crozers.

The exhilaration of their exploits seemed to haunt the memories of their descendants alone, and the shame to be forgotten. Pride glowed in their bosoms to publish their relationship to "Andrew Ellwald of the Laverockstanes, called Ùnchancy Dand,' who was justifeed wi' seeven mair of the same name at Jeddart in the days of King James the Sax." In all this tissue of crime and misfortune, the Elliotts of Cauldstaneslap had one boast which must appear legitimate: the males were gallows-birds, born outlaws, petty thieves, and deadly brawlers; but, according to the same tradition, the females were all chaste and faithful.

The power of ancestry on the character is not limited to the inheritance of cells. If I buy ancestors by the gross from the benevolence of Lyon King of Arms, my grandson (if he is Scottish) will feel a quickening emulation of their deeds. The men of the Elliotts were proud, lawless, violent as of right, cherishing and prolonging a tradition. In like manner with the women. And the woman, essentially passionate and reckless, who crouched on the rug, in the shine of the peat fire, telling these tales, had cherished through life a wild integrity of virtue.

Her father Gilbert had been deeply pious, a savage disciplinarian in the antique style, and withal a notorious smuggler. "I mind when I was a bairn getting mony a skelp and being shoo'd to bed like pou'try," she would say. "That would be when the lads and their bit kegs were on the road. We've had the riffraff of two-three counties in our kitchen, mony's the time, betwix' the twelve and the three; and their lanterns would be standing in the forecourt, ay, a score o' them at once. But there was nae ungodly talk permitted at Cauldstaneslap. My faither was a consistent man in walk and conversation; just let slip an aith, and there was the door to ye! He had that zeal for the Lord, it was a fair wonder to hear him pray, but the family has aye had a gift that way."

This father was twice married, once to a dark woman of the old Ellwald stock, by whom he had Gilbert, presently of Cauldstaneslap; and, secondly, to the mother of Kirstie. "He was an auld man when he married her, a fell auld man wi' a muckle voice - you could hear him rowting from the top o' the Kye-skairs," she said; "but for her, it appears she was a perfit wonder. It was gentle blood she had, Mr.

Archie, for it was your ain. The country-side gaed gyte about her and her gowden hair.

Mines is no to be mentioned wi' it, and there's few weemen has mair hair than what I have, or yet a bonnier colour. Often would I tell my dear Miss Jeannie - that was your mother, dear, she was cruel ta'en up about her hair, it was unco' tender, ye see - 'Houts, Miss Jeannie,' I would say, 'just fling your washes and your French dentifrishes in the back o'

the fire, for that's the place for them; and awa' down to a burn side, and wash yersel' in cauld hill water, and dry your bonny hair in the caller wind o' the muirs, the way that my mother aye washed hers, and page 71 / 166

that I have aye made it a practice to have wishen mines - just you do what I tell ye, my dear, and ye'll give me news of it! Ye'll have hair, and routh of hair, a pigtail as thick's my arm,' I said, ànd the bonniest colour like the clear gowden guineas, so as the lads in kirk'll no can keep their eyes off it!' Weel, it lasted out her time, puir thing! I cuttit a lock of it upon her corp that was lying there sae cauld. I'll show it ye some of thir days if ye're good. But, as I was sayin', my mither - "

On the death of the father there remained golden-haired Kirstie, who took service with her distant kinsfolk, the Rutherfords, and black-avised Gilbert, twenty years older, who farmed the Cauldstaneslap, married, and begot four sons between 1773 and 1784, and a daughter, like a postscript, in '97, the year of Camperdown and Cape St. Vincent. It seemed it was a tradition in the family to wind up with a belated girl.

In 1804, at the age of sixty, Gilbert met an end that might be called heroic. He was due home from market any time from eight at night till five in the morning, and in any condition from the quarrelsome to the speechless, for he maintained to that age the goodly customs of the Scots farmer. It was known on this occasion that he had a good bit of money to bring home; the word had gone round loosely. The laird had shown his guineas, and if anybody had but noticed it, there was an ill-looking, vagabond crew, the scum of Edinburgh, that drew out of the market long ere it was dusk and took the hill-road by Hermiston, where it was not to be believed that they had lawful business. One of the country-side, one Dickieson, they took with them to be their guide, and dear he paid for it! Of a sudden in the ford of the Broken Dykes, this page 72 / 166

vermin clan fell on the laird, six to one, and him three parts asleep, having drunk hard. But it is ill to catch an Elliott.

For a while, in the night and the black water that was deep as to his saddle-girths, he wrought with his staff like a smith at his stithy, and great was the sound of oaths and blows. With that the ambuscade was burst, and he rode for home with a pistol-ball in him, three knife wounds, the loss of his front teeth, a broken rib and bridle, and a dying horse. That was a race with death that the laird rode! In the mirk night, with his broken bridle and his head swimming, he dug his spurs to the rowels in the horse's side, and the horse, that was even worse off than himself, the poor creature! screamed out loud like a person as he went, so that the hills echoed with it, and the folks at Cauldstaneslap got to their feet about the table and looked at each other with white faces. The horse fell dead at the yard gate, the laird won the length of the house and fell there on the threshold. To the son that raised him he gave the bag of money. "Hae," said he. All the way up the thieves had seemed to him to be at his heels, but now the hallucination left him - he saw them again in the place of the ambuscade

- and the thirst of vengeance seized on his dying mind. Raising himself and pointing with an imperious finger into the black night from which he had come, he uttered the single command, "Brocken Dykes," and fainted.

He had never been loved, but he had been feared in honour. At that sight, at that word, gasped out at them from a toothless and bleeding mouth, the old Elliott spirit awoke with a shout in the four sons.

"Wanting the hat," continues my author, Kirstie, whom I but haltingly follow, for she told this tale like one inspired, "wanting guns, for there wasna twa grains o' pouder in the house, wi' nae mair weepons than their sticks into their hands, the fower o' them took the road. Only page 73 / 166

Hob, and that was the eldest, hunkered at the doorsill where the blood had rin, fyled his hand wi' it - and haddit it up to Heeven in the way o' the auld Border aith. `Hell shall have her ain again this nicht!' he raired, and rode forth upon his earrand." It was three miles to Broken Dykes, down hill, and a sore road. Kirstie has seen men from Edinburgh dismounting there in plain day to lead their horses. But the four brothers rode it as if Auld Hornie were behind and Heaven in front.

Come to the ford, and there was Dickieson. By all tales, he was not dead, but breathed and reared upon his elbow, and cried out to them for help. It was at a graceless face that he asked mercy. As soon as Hob saw, by the glint of the lantern, the eyes shining and the whiteness of the teeth in the man's face, "Damn you!" says he; "ye hae your teeth, hae ye?" and rode his horse to and fro upon that human remnant. Beyond that, Dandie must dismount with the lantern to be their guide; he was the youngest son, scarce twenty at the time. "A' nicht long they gaed in the wet heath and jennipers, and whaur they gaed they neither knew nor cared, but just followed the bluid stains and the footprints o'

their faither's murderers. And a' nicht Dandie had his nose to the grund like a tyke, and the ithers followed and spak' naething, neither black nor white. There was nae noise to be heard, but just the sough of the swalled burns, and Hob, the dour yin, risping his teeth as he gaed."

With the first glint of the morning they saw they were on the drove road, and at that the four stopped and had a dram to their breakfasts, for they knew that Dand must have guided them right, and the rogues could be but little ahead, hot foot for Edinburgh by the way of the Pentland Hills. By eight o'clock they had word of them - a shepherd had seen four men "uncoly mishandled" go by in the last hour. "That's yin a piece," says Clem, and swung his cudgel. "Five o' them!" says Hob.

"God's death, but the faither was a man! And him drunk!" And then there befell them what my author termed "a sair misbegowk," for they were overtaken by a posse of mounted neighbours come to aid in the pursuit. Four sour faces looked on the reinforcement. "The Deil's broughten you!" said Clem, and they rode thenceforward in the rear of the party with hanging heads. Before ten they had found and secured the rogues, and by three of the afternoon, as they rode up the Vennel with their prisoners, they were aware of a concourse of people bearing in their midst something that dripped. "For the boady of the saxt,"

pursued Kirstie, "wi' his head smashed like a hazelnit, had been a' that nicht in the chairge o' Hermiston Water, and it dunting it on the stanes, and grunding it on the shallows, and flinging the deid thing heels-ower-hurdie at the Fa's o'

Spango; and in the first o' the day, Tweed had got a hold o' him and carried him off like a wind, for it was uncoly swalled, and raced wi' him, bobbing under brae-sides, and was long playing with the creature in the drumlie lynns under the castle, and at the hinder end of all cuist him up on the starling of Crossmichael brig. Sae there they were a'thegither at last (for Dickieson had been brought in on a cart long syne), and folk could see what mainner o'man my brither had been that had held his head again sax and saved the siller, and him drunk!" Thus died of honourable injuries and in the savour of fame Gilbert Elliott of the Cauldstaneslap; but his sons had scarce less glory out of the business. Their savage haste, the skill with which Dand had found and followed the trail, the barbarity to the wounded Dickieson (which was like an open secret in the county), and the doom which it was currently supposed they had intended for the others, struck and stirred popular imagination. Some century earlier the last of the minstrels might have fashioned the last of the ballads page 75 / 166

out of that Homeric fight and chase; but the spirit was dead, or had been reincarnated already in Mr. Sheriff Scott, and the degenerate moorsmen must be content to tell the tale in prose, and to make of the

"Four Black Brothers" a unit after the fashion of the "Twelve Apostles"

or the "Three Musketeers."

Robert, Gilbert, Clement, and Andrew - in the proper Border diminutives, Hob, Gib, Clem, and Dand Elliott - these ballad heroes, had much in common; in particular, their high sense of the family and the family honour; but they went diverse ways, and prospered and failed in different businesses. According to Kirstie, "they had a' bees in their bonnets but Hob." Hob the laird was, indeed, essentially a decent man.

An elder of the Kirk, nobody had heard an oath upon his lips, save perhaps thrice or so at the sheep-washing, since the chase of his father's murderers. The figure he had shown on that eventful night disappeared as if swallowed by a trap. He who had ecstatically dipped his hand in the red blood, he who had ridden down Dickieson, became, from that moment on, a stiff and rather graceless model of the rustic proprieties; cannily profiting by the high war prices, and yearly stowing away a little nest-egg in the bank against calamity; approved of and sometimes consulted by the greater lairds for the massive and placid sense of what he said, when he could be induced to say anything; and particularly valued by the minister, Mr. Torrance, as a right-hand man in the parish, and a model to parents. The transfiguration had been for the moment only; some Barbarossa, some old Adam of our ancestors, sleeps in all of us till the fit circumstance shall call it into action; and, for as sober as he now seemed, Hob had given once for all the measure of page 76 / 166

the devil that haunted him. He was married, and, by reason of the effulgence of that legendary night, was adored by his wife.

He had a mob of little lusty, barefoot children who marched in a caravan the long miles to school, the stages of whose pilgrimage were marked by acts of spoliation and mischief, and who were qualified in the country-side as "fair pests." But in the house, if "faither was in," they were quiet as mice. In short, Hob moved through life in a great peace - the reward of any one who shall have killed his man, with any formidable and figurative circumstance, in the midst of a country gagged and swaddled with civilisation.

It was a current remark that the Elliotts were "guid and bad, like sanguishes"; and certainly there was a curious distinction, the men of business coming alternately with the dreamers. The second brother, Gib, was a weaver by trade, had gone out early into the world to Edinburgh, and come home again with his wings singed. There was an exaltation in his nature which had led him to embrace with enthusiasm the principles of the French Revolution, and had ended by bringing him under the hawse of my Lord Hermiston in that furious onslaught of his upon the Liberals, which sent Muir and Palmer into exile and dashed the party into chaff.

It was whispered that my lord, in his great scorn for the movement, and prevailed upon a little by a sense of neighbourliness, had given Gib a hint. Meeting him one day in the Potterrow, my lord had stopped in front of him: "Gib, ye eediot," he had said, "what's this I hear of you?

Poalitics, poalitics, poalitics, weaver's poalitics, is the way of it, I hear. If ye arena a'thegither dozened with cediocy, ye'll gang your ways back to Cauldstaneslap, and ca' your loom, and ca' your loom, man!"

And Gilbert had taken him at the word and returned, with an expedition almost to be called flight, to the house of his father. The clearest of his inheritance was that family gift of prayer of which Kirstie had boasted; and the baffled politician now turned his attention to religious matters - or, as others said, to heresy and schism. Every Sunday morning he was in Crossmichael, where he had gathered together, one by one, a sect of about a dozen persons, who called themselves

"God's Remnant of the True Faithful," or, for short, "God's Remnant."

To the profane, they were known as "Gib's Deils." Bailie Sweedie, a noted humorist in the town, vowed that the proceedings always opened to the tune of "The Deil Fly Away with the Exciseman," and that the sacrament was dispensed in the form of hot whisky-toddy; both wicked hits at the evangelist, who had been suspected of smuggling in his youth, and had been overtaken (as the phrase went) on the streets of Crossmichael one Fair day. It was known that every Sunday they prayed for a blessing on the arms of Bonaparte. For this "God's Remnant," as they were "skailing" from the cottage that did duty for a temple, had been repeatedly stoned by the bairns, and Gib himself hooted by a squadron of Border volunteers in which his own brother, Dand, rode in a uniform and with a drawn sword. The "Remnant" were believed, besides, to be "antinomian in principle," which might otherwise have been a serious charge, but the way public opinion then blew it was quite swallowed up and forgotten in the scandal about Bonaparte. For the rest, Gilbert had set up his loom in an outhouse at Cauldstaneslap, where he laboured assiduously six days of the week. His brothers, appalled by his political opinions, and willing to avoid dissension in the household, spoke but little to him; he less to them, remaining absorbed in the study of the Bible and almost constant prayer. The page 78 / 166

gaunt weaver was dry-nurse at Cauldstaneslap, and the bairns loved him dearly. Except when he was carrying an infant in his arms, he was rarely seen to smile - as, indeed, there were few smilers in that family. When his sister-in-law rallied him, and proposed that he should get a wife and bairns of his own, since he was so fond of them, "I have no clearness of mind upon that point," he would reply. If nobody called him in to dinner, he stayed out. Mrs. Hob, a hard, unsympathetic woman, once tried the experiment. He went without food all day, but at dusk, as the light began to fail him, he came into the house of his own accord, looking puzzled. "I've had a great gale of prayer upon my speerit," said he. "I canna mind sae muckle's what I had for denner."

The creed of God's Remnant was justified in the life of its founder.

"And yet I dinna ken," said Kirstie. "He's maybe no more stockfish than his neeghbours! He rode wi' the rest o' them, and had a good stamach to the work, by a' that I hear! God's Remnant! The deil's clavers! There wasna muckle Christianity in the way Hob guided Johnny Dickieson, at the least of it; but Guid kens! Is he a Christian even? He might be a Mahommedan or a Deevil or a Fire-worshipper, for what I ken."

The third brother had his name on a door-plate, no less, in the city of Glasgow, "Mr. Clement Elliott," as long as your arm. In his case, that spirit of innovation which had shown itself timidly in the case of Hob by the admission of new manures, and which had run to waste with Gilbert in subversive politics and heretical religions, bore useful fruit in many ingenious mechanical improvements. In boyhood, from his addiction to strange devices of sticks and string, he had been counted the most eccentric of the family. But that was all by now; and he was a partner page 79 / 166

of his firm, and looked to die a bailie. He too had married, and was rearing a plentiful family in the smoke and din of Glasgow; he was wealthy, and could have bought out his brother, the cock-laird, six times over, it was whispered;

and when he slipped away to Cauldstaneslap for a well-earned holiday, which he did as often as he was able, he astonished the neighbours with his broadcloth, his beaver hat, and the ample plies of his neckcloth. Though an eminently solid man at bottom, after the pattern of Hob, he had contracted a certain Glasgow briskness and APLOMB which set him off. All the other Elliotts were as lean as a rake, but Clement was laying on fat, and he panted sorely when he must get into his boots. Dand said, chuckling: "Ay, Clem has the elements of a corporation." "A provost and corporation," returned Clem. And his readiness was much admired.

The fourth brother, Dand, was a shepherd to his trade, and by starts, when he could bring his mind to it, excelled in the business. Nobody could train a dog like Dandie; nobody, through the peril of great storms in the winter time, could do more gallantly. But if his dexterity were exquisite, his diligence was but fitful; and he served his brother for bed and board, and a trifle of pocket-money when he asked for it. He loved money well enough, knew very well how to spend it, and could make a shrewd bargain when he liked. But he preferred a vague knowledge that he was well to windward to any counted coins in the pocket; he felt himself richer so. Hob would expostulate: "I'm an amature herd." Dand would reply, "I'll keep your sheep to you when I'm so minded, but I'll keep my liberty too. Thir's no man can coandescend on what I'm worth."

Clein would expound to him the miraculous results of compound interest, page 80 / 166

and recommend investments. "Ay, man?" Dand would say; "and do you think, if I took Hob's siller, that I wouldna drink it or wear it on the lassies? And, anyway, my kingdom is no of this world. Either I'm a poet or else I'm nothing." Clem would remind him of old age. "I'll die young, like, Robbie Burns," he would say stoutly. No question but he had a certain accomplishment in minor verse. His "Hermiston Burn," with its pretty refrain -

"I love to gang thinking whaur ye gang linking, Hermiston burn, in the howe;"

his "Auld, auld Elliotts, clay-cauld Elliotts, dour, bauld Elliotts of auld," and his really fascinating piece about the Praying Weaver's Stone, had gained him in the neighbourhood the reputation, still possible in Scotland, of a local bard; and, though not printed himself, he was recognised by others who were and who had become famous. Walter Scott owed to Dandie the text of the "Raid of Wearie" in the MINSTRELSY; and made him welcome at his house, and appreciated his talents, such as they were, with all his usual generosity. The Ettrick Shepherd was his sworn crony; they would meet, drink to excess, roar out their lyrics in each other's faces, and quarrel and make it up again till bedtime. And besides these recognitions, almost to be called official, Dandie was made welcome for the sake of his gift through the farmhouses of several contiguous dales, and was thus exposed to manifold temptations which he rather sought than fled. He had figured on the stool of repentance, for once fulfilling to the letter the tradition of his hero and model. His humorous verses to Mr. Torrance on that occasion - "Kenspeckle here my page 81 / 166

lane I stand" - unfortunately too indelicate for further citation, ran through the country like a fiery cross - they were recited, quoted, paraphrased, and laughed over as far away as Dumfries on the one hand and Dunbar on the other.

These four brothers were united by a close bond, the bond of that mutual admiration - or rather mutual hero-worship - which is so strong among the members of secluded families who have much ability and little culture. Even the extremes admired each other. Hob, who had as much poetry as the tongs, professed to find pleasure in Dand's verses; Clem, who had no more religion than Claverhouse, nourished a heartfelt, at least an open-mouthed, admiration of Gib's prayers; and Dandie followed with relish the rise of Clem's fortunes. Indulgence followed hard on the heels of admiration. The laird, Clem, and Dand, who were Tories and patriots of the hottest quality, excused to themselves, with a certain bashfulness, the radical and revolutionary heresies of Gib. By another division of the family, the laird, Clem, and Gib, who were men exactly virtuous, swallowed the dose of Dand's irregularities as a kind of clog or drawback in the mysterious providence of God affixed to bards, and distinctly probative of poetical genius. To appreciate the simplicity of their mutual admiration it was necessary to hear Clem, arrived upon one of his visits, and dealing in a spirit of continuous irony with the affairs and personalities of that great city of Glasgow where he lived and transacted business. The various personages, ministers of the church, municipal officers, mercantile big-wigs, whom he had occasion to introduce, were all alike denigrated, all served but as reflectors to cast back a flattering side-light on the house of Cauldstaneslap. The

Provost, for whom Clem by exception entertained a measure of respect, he would liken to Hob. "He minds me o' the laird there," he would say. "He has some of Hob's grand, whunstane sense, and the same way with him of steiking his mouth when he's no very pleased." And Hob, all unconscious, would draw down his upper lip and produce, as if for comparison, the formidable grimace referred to. The unsatisfactory incumbent of St. Enoch's Kirk was thus briefly dismissed: "If he had but twa fingers o' Gib's, he would waken them up." And Gib, honest man! would look down and secretly smile. Clem was a spy whom they had sent out into the world of men. He had come back with the good news that there was nobody to compare with the Four Black Brothers, no position that they would not adorn, no official that it would not be well they should replace, no interest of mankind, secular or spiritual, which would not immediately bloom under their supervision. The excuse of their folly is in two words: scarce the breadth of a hair divided them from the peasantry. The measure of their sense is this: that these symposia of rustic vanity were kept entirely within the family, like some secret ancestral practice. To the world their serious faces were never deformed by the suspicion of any simper of self-contentment. Yet it was known. "They hae a guid pride o' themsel's!" was the word in the country-side.

Lastly, in a Border story, there should be added their "two-names." Hob was The Laird. "Roy ne puis, prince ne daigne"; he was the laird of Cauldstaneslap - say fifty acres - IPSISSIMUS. Clement was Mr. Elliott, as upon his door-plate, the earlier Dafty having been discarded as no longer applicable, and indeed only a reminder of misjudgment and the page 83 / 166

imbecility of the public; and the youngest, in honour of his perpetual wanderings, was known by the sobriquet of Randy Dand.

It will be understood that not all this information was communicated by the aunt, who had too much of the family failing herself to appreciate it thoroughly in others.

But as time went on, Archie began to observe an omission in the family chronicle.

"Is there not a girl too?" he asked.

"Ay: Kirstie. She was named for me, or my grandmother at least - it's the same thing," returned the aunt, and went on again about Dand, whom she secretly preferred by reason of his gallantries.

"But what is your niece like?" said Archie at the next opportunity.

"Her? As black's your hat! But I dinna suppose she would maybe be what you would ca' ILL-LOOKED a'thegither. Na, she's a kind of a handsome jaud - a kind o' gipsy," said the aunt, who had two sets of scales for men and women - or perhaps it would be more fair to say that she had three, and the third and the most loaded was for girls.

"How comes it that I never see her in church?" said Archie.

" 'Deed, and I believe she's in Glesgie with Clem and his wife. A heap good she's like to get of it! I dinna say for men folk, but where weemen folk are born, there let them bide. Glory to God, I was never far'er from here than Crossmichael."

In the meanwhile it began to strike Archie as strange, that while she thus sang the praises of her kinsfolk, and manifestly relished their virtues and (I may say) their vices like a thing creditable to herself, there should appear not the least sign of cordiality between the house of Hermiston and that of Cauldstaneslap. Going to church of a Sunday, as the lady housekeeper stepped with her skirts kilted, three tucks of her white petticoat showing below, and her best India shawl upon her back (if the day were fine) in a pattern of radiant dyes, she would sometimes overtake her relatives preceding her more leisurely in the same direction. Gib of course was absent: by skreigh of day he had been gone to Crossmichael and his fellow-heretics; but the rest of the family would be seen marching in open order: Hob and Dand, stiff-necked, straight-backed six-footers, with severe dark faces, and their plaids about their shoulders; the convoy of children scattering (in a state of high polish) on the wayside, and every now and again collected by the shrill summons of the mother; and the mother herself, by a suggestive circumstance which might have afforded matter of thought to a more experienced observer than Archie, wrapped in a shawl nearly identical with Kirstie's, but a thought more gaudy and conspicuously newer. At the sight, Kirstie grew more tall - Kirstie showed her classical profile, nose in air and nostril spread, the pure blood came in her cheek evenly in a delicate living pink.

"A braw day to ye, Mistress Elliott," said she, and hostility and gentility were nicely mingled in her tones. "A fine day, mem," the laird's wife would reply with a miraculous curtsey, spreading the while her plumage - setting off, in other words, and with arts unknown to the mere man, the pattern of her India shawl. Behind her, the whole Cauldstaneslap contingent marched in closer order, and with an indescribable air of being in the presence of the foe; and while Dandie saluted his aunt with a certain familiarity as of one who was well in court, Hob marched on in awful immobility. There appeared upon the face of this attitude in the family the consequences of some dreadful feud.

Presumably the two women had been principals in the original encounter, and the laird had probably been drawn into the quarrel by the ears, too late to be included in the present skin-deep reconciliation.

"Kirstie," said Archie one day, "what is this you have against your family?"

"I dinna complean," said Kirstie, with a flush. "I say naething."

"I see you do not - not even good-day to your own nephew," said he.

"I hae naething to be ashamed of," said she. "I can say the Lord's prayer with a good grace. If Hob was ill, or in preeson or poverty, I would see to him blithely. But for curtchying and complimenting and page 86 / 166

colloguing, thank ye kindly!"

Archie had a bit of a smile: he leaned back in his chair. "I think you and Mrs. Robert are not very good friends," says he slyly, "when you have your India shawls on?"

She looked upon him in silence, with a sparkling eye but an indecipherable expression; and that was all that Archie was ever destined to learn of the battle of the India shawls.

"Do none of them ever come here to see you?" he inquired.

"Mr. Archie," said she, "I hope that I ken my place better. It would be a queer thing, I think, if I was to clamjamfry up your faither's house -

that I should say it! - wi' a dirty, black-a-vised clan, no ane o' them it was worth while to mar soap upon but just mysel'! Na, they're all damnifeed wi' the black Ellwalds. I have nae patience wi' black folk."

Then, with a sudden consciousness of the case of Archie, "No that it maitters for men sae muckle," she made haste to add, "but there's naebody can deny that it's unwomanly. Long hair is the ornament o'

woman ony way; we've good warrandise for that - it's in the Bible - and wha can doubt that the Apostle had some gowden-haired lassie in his mind

- Apostle and all, for what was he but just a man like yersel'?"

CHAPTER VI - A LEAF FROM CHRISTINA'S PSALM-BOOK

ARCHIE was sedulous at church. Sunday after Sunday he sat down and stood up with that small company, heard the voice of Mr. Torrance leaping like an ill-played clarionet from key to key, and had an opportunity to study his moth-eaten gown and the black thread mittens that he joined together in prayer, and lifted up with a reverent solemnity in the act of benediction. Hermiston pew was a little square box, dwarfish in proportion with the kirk itself, and enclosing a table not much bigger than a footstool. There sat Archie, an apparent prince, the only undeniable gentleman and the only great heritor in the parish, taking his ease in the only pew, for no other in the kirk had doors.

Thence he might command an undisturbed view of that congregation of solid plaided men, strapping wives and daughters, oppressed children, and uneasy sheep-dogs. It was strange how Archie missed the look of race; except the dogs, with their refined foxy faces and inimitably curling tails, there was no one present with the least claim to gentility. The Cauldstaneslap party was scarcely an exception; Dandie perhaps, as he amused himself making verses through the interminable burden of the service, stood out a little by the glow in his eye and a certain superior animation of face and alertness of body; but even Dandie slouched like a rustic. The rest of the congregation, like so many sheep, oppressed him with a sense of hobnailed routine, day following day - of physical labour in the open air, oatmeal porridge, peas bannock the somnolent fireside in the evening, and the night-long nasal slumbers in a box-bed. Yet he knew many of them to be shrewd and humorous, men of character, notable women, making a bustle in the world and radiating an influence from their low-browed doors. He knew besides page 88 / 166

they were like other men; below the crust of custom, rapture found a way; he had heard them beat the timbrel before Bacchus - had heard them shout and carouse over their whisky-toddy; and not the most Dutch-bottomed and severe faces among them all, not even the solemn elders themselves, but were capable of singular gambols at the voice of love.

Men drawing near to an end of life's adventurous journey - maids thrilling with fear and curiosity on the threshold of entrance - women who had borne and perhaps buried children, who could remember the clinging of the small dead hands and the patter of the little feet now silent - he marvelled that among all those faces there should be no face of expectation, none that was mobile, none into which the rhythm and poetry of life had entered. "O for a live face," he thought; and at times he had a memory of Lady Flora; and at times he would study the living gallery before him with despair, and would see himself go on to waste his days in that joyless pastoral place, and death come to him, and his grave be dug under the rowans, and the Spirit of the Earth laugh out in a thunder-peal at the huge fiasco.

On this particular Sunday, there was no doubt but that the spring had come at last. It was warm, with a latent shiver in the air that made the warmth only the more welcome. The shallows of the stream glittered and tinkled among bunches of primrose. Vagrant scents of the earth arrested Archie by the way with moments of ethereal intoxication. The grey Quakerish dale was still only awakened in places and patches from the sobriety of its winter colouring; and he wondered at its beauty; an essential beauty of the old earth it seemed to him, not resident in particulars but breathing to him from the whole. He surprised himself

by a sudden impulse to write poetry - he did so sometimes, loose, galloping octo-syllabics in the vein of Scott - and when he had taken his place on a boulder, near some fairy falls and shaded by a whip of a tree that was already radiant with new leaves, it still more surprised him that he should have nothing to write. His heart perhaps beat in time to some vast indwelling rhythm of the universe. By the time he came to a corner of the valley and could see the kirk, he had so lingered by the way that the first psalm was finishing. The nasal psalmody, full of turns and trills and graceless graces, seemed the essential voice of the kirk itself upraised in thanksgiving,

"Everything's alive," he said; and again cries it aloud, "thank God, everything's alive!" He lingered yet a while in the kirk-yard. A tuft of primroses was blooming hard by the leg of an old black table tombstone, and he stopped to contemplate the random apologue. They stood forth on the cold earth with a trenchancy of contrast; and he was struck with a sense of incompleteness in the day, the season, and the beauty that surrounded him - the chill there was in the warmth, the gross black clods about the opening primroses, the damp earthy smell that was everywhere intermingled with the scents. The voice of the aged Torrance within rose in an ecstasy. And he wondered if Torrance also felt in his old bones the joyous influence of the spring morning; Torrance, or the shadow of what once was Torrance, that must come so soon to lie outside here in the sun and rain with all his rheumatisms, while a new minister stood in his room and thundered from his own familiar pulpit? The pity of it, and something of the chill of the grave, shook him for a moment as he made haste to enter.

page 90 / 166

He went up the aisle reverently, and took his place in the pew with lowered eyes, for he feared he had already offended the kind old gentleman in the pulpit, and was sedulous to offend no further. He could not follow the prayer, not even the heads of it. Brightnesses of azure, clouds of fragrance, a tinkle of falling water and singing birds, rose like exhalations from some deeper, aboriginal memory, that was not his, but belonged to the flesh on his bones. His body remembered; and it seemed to him that his body was in no way gross, but ethereal and perishable like a strain of music; and he felt for it an exquisite tenderness as for a child, an innocent, full of beautiful instincts and destined to an early death. And he felt for old Torrance

- of the many supplications, of the few days - a pity that was near to tears. The prayer ended. Right over him was a tablet in the wall, the only ornament in the roughly masoned chapel - for it was no more; the tablet commemorated, I was about to say the virtues, but rather the existence of a former Rutherford of Hermiston; and Archie, under that trophy of his long descent and local greatness, leaned back in the pew and contemplated vacancy with the shadow of a smile between playful and sad, that became him strangely. Dandie's sister, sitting by the side of Clem in her new Glasgow finery, chose that moment to observe the young laird. Aware of the stir of his entrance, the little formalist had kept her eyes fastened and her face prettily composed during the prayer. It was not hypocrisy, there was no one further from a hypocrite. The girl had been taught to behave: to look up, to look down, to look unconscious, to look seriously impressed in church, and in every conjuncture to look her best. That was the game of female life, and she played it frankly. Archie was the one person in church who was of interest, who was somebody new, reputed eccentric, known to be young,

and a laird, and still unseen by Christina. Small wonder that, as she stood there in her attitude of pretty decency, her mind should run upon him! If he spared a glance in her direction, he should know she was a well-behaved young lady who had been to Glasgow. In reason he must admire her clothes, and it was possible that he should think her pretty. At that her heart beat the least thing in the world; and she proceeded, by way of a corrective, to call up and dismiss a series of fancied pictures of the young man who should now, by rights, be looking at her. She settled on the plainest of them, - a pink short young man with a dish face and no figure, at whose admiration she could afford to smile; but for all that, the consciousness of his gaze (which was really fixed on Torrance and his mittens) kept her in something of a flutter till the word Amen. Even then, she was far too well-bred to gratify her curiosity with any impatience. She resumed her seat languidly - this was a Glasgow touch - she composed her dress, rearranged her nosegay of primroses, looked first in front, then behind upon the other side, and at last allowed her eyes to move, without hurry, in the direction of the Hermiston pew. For a moment, they were riveted. Next she had plucked her gaze home again like a tame bird who should have meditated flight. Possibilities crowded on her; she hung over the future and grew dizzy; the image of this young man, slim, graceful, dark, with the inscrutable half-smile, attracted and repelled her like a chasm. "I wonder, will I have met my fate?" she thought, and her heart swelled.

Torrance was got some way into his first exposition, positing a deep layer of texts as he went along, laying the foundations of his discourse, which was to deal with a nice point in divinity, before page 92 / 166

Archie suffered his eyes to wander. They fell first of all on Clem, looking insupportably prosperous, and patronising Torrance with the favour of a modified attention, as of one who was used to better things in Glasgow. Though he had never before set eyes on him, Archie had no difficulty in identifying him, and no hesitation in pronouncing him vulgar, the worst of the family. Clem was leaning lazily forward when Archie first saw him. Presently he leaned nonchalantly back; and that deadly instrument, the maiden, was suddenly unmasked in profile. Though not quite in the front of the fashion (had anybody cared!), certain artful Glasgow mantua-makers, and her own inherent taste, had arrayed her to great advantage. Her accoutrement was, indeed, a cause of heart-burning, and almost of scandal, in that infinitesimal kirk company.

Mrs. Hob had said her say at Cauldstaneslap. "Daft-like!" she had pronounced it. "A jaiket that'll no meet! Whaur's the sense of a jaiket that'll no button upon you, if it should come to be weet? What do ye ca' thir things? Demmy brokens, d'ye say? They'll be brokens wi' a vengeance or ye can win back! Weel, I have nae thing to do wi' it -

it's no good taste." Clem, whose purse had thus metamorphosed his sister, and who was not insensible to the advertisement, had come to the rescue with a "Hoot, woman! What do you ken of good taste that has never been to the ceety?" And Hob, looking on the girl with pleased smiles, as she timidly displayed her finery in the midst of the dark kitchen, had thus ended the dispute: "The cutty looks weel," he had said, "and it's no very like rain. Wear them the day, hizzie; but it's no a thing to make a practice o'." In the breasts of her rivals, coming to the kirk very conscious of white under-linen, and their faces splendid with much soap, the sight of the toilet had raised a storm of varying emotion, from the mere unenvious admiration that was expressed page 93 / 166

in a long-drawn "Eh!" to the angrier feeling that found vent in an emphatic "Set her up!" Her frock was of straw-coloured jaconet muslin, cut low at the bosom and short at the ankle, so as to display her DEMI-BROQUINS of Regency violet, crossing with many straps upon a yellow cobweb stocking. According to the pretty fashion in which our grandmothers did not hesitate to appear, and our great-aunts went forth armed for the pursuit and capture of our great-uncles, the dress was drawn up so as to mould the contour of both breasts, and in the nook between, a cairngorm brooch maintained it. Here, too, surely in a very enviable position, trembled the nosegay of primroses. She wore on her shoulders - or rather on her back and not her shoulders, which it scarcely passed - a French coat of sarsenet, tied in front with Margate braces, and of the same colour with her violet shoes. About her face clustered a disorder of dark ringlets, a little garland of yellow French roses surmounted her brow, and the whole was crowned by a village hat of chipped straw. Amongst all the rosy and all the weathered faces that surrounded her in church, she glowed like an open flower - girl and raiment, and the cairngorm that caught the daylight and returned it in a fiery flash, and the threads of bronze and gold that played in her hair.

Archie was attracted by the bright thing like a child. He looked at her again and yet again, and their looks crossed. The lip was lifted from her little teeth. He saw the red blood work vividly under her tawny skin. Her eye, which was great as a stag's, struck and held his gaze.

He knew who she must be - Kirstie, she of the harsh diminutive, his housekeeper's niece, the sister of the rustic prophet, Gib - and he found in her the answer to his wishes.

Christina felt the shock of their encountering glances, and seemed to rise, clothed in smiles, into a region of the vague and bright. But the gratification was not more exquisite than it was brief. She looked away abruptly, and immediately began to blame herself for that abruptness.

She knew what she should have done, too late - turned slowly with her nose in the air. And meantime his look was not removed, but continued to play upon her like a battery of cannon constantly aimed, and now seemed to isolate her alone with him, and now seemed to uplift her, as on a pillory, before the congregation. For Archie continued to drink her in with his eyes, even as a wayfarer comes to a well-head on a mountain, and stoops his face, and drinks with thirst unassuageable. In the cleft of her little breasts the fiery eye of the topaz and the pale florets of primrose fascinated him. He saw the breasts heave, and the flowers shake with the heaving, and marvelled what should so much discompose the girl. And Christina was conscious of his gaze - saw it, perhaps, with the dainty plaything of an ear that peeped among her ringlets; she was conscious of changing colour, conscious of her unsteady breath. Like a creature tracked, run down, surrounded, she sought in a dozen ways to give herself a countenance. She used her handkerchief - it was a really fine one - then she desisted in a panic:

"He would only think I was too warm." She took to reading in the metrical psalms, and then remembered it was sermon-time. Last she put a

"sugar-bool" in her mouth, and the next moment repented of the step. It was such a homely-like thing! Mr. Archie would never be eating sweeties in kirk; and, with a palpable effort, she swallowed it whole, and her colour flamed high. At this signal of distress Archie awoke to a sense page 95 / 166

of his ill-behaviour. What had he been doing? He had been exquisitely rude in church to the niece of his housekeeper; he had stared like a lackey and a libertine at a beautiful and modest girl. It was possible, it was even likely, he would be presented to her after service in the kirk-yard, and then how was he to look? And there was no excuse. He had marked the tokens of her shame, of her increasing indignation, and he was such a fool that he had not understood them. Shame bowed him down, and he looked resolutely at Mr. Torrance; who little supposed, good, worthy man, as he continued to expound justification by faith, what was his true business: to play the part of derivative to a pair of children at the old game of falling in love.

Christina was greatly relieved at first. It seemed to her that she was clothed again. She looked back on what had passed. All would have been right if she had not blushed, a silly fool! There was nothing to blush at, if she HAD taken a sugar-bool. Mrs. MacTaggart, the elder's wife in St. Enoch's, took them often. And if he had looked at her, what was more natural than that a young gentleman should look at the best-dressed girl in church? And at the same time, she knew far otherwise, she knew there was nothing casual or ordinary in the look, and valued herself on its memory like a decoration. Well, it was a blessing he had found something else to look at! And presently she began to have other thoughts. It was necessary, she fancied, that she should put herself right by a repetition of the incident, better managed. If the wish was father to the thought, she did not know or she would not recognise it.

It was simply as a manoeuvre of propriety, as something called for to lessen the significance of what had gone before, that she should a page 96 / 166

second time meet his eyes, and this time without blushing. And at the memory of the blush, she blushed again, and became one general blush burning from head to foot. Was ever anything so indelicate, so forward, done by a girl before? And here she was, making an exhibition of herself before the congregation about nothing! She stole a glance upon her neighbours, and behold! they were steadily indifferent, and Clem had gone to sleep. And still the one idea was becoming more and more potent with her, that in common prudence she must look again before the service ended. Something of the same sort was going forward in the mind of Archie, as he struggled with the load of penitence. So it chanced that, in the flutter of the moment when the last psalm was given out, and Torrance was reading the verse, and the leaves of every psalm-book in church were rustling under busy fingers, two stealthy glances were sent out like antennae among the pews and on the indifferent and absorbed occupants, and drew timidly nearer to the straight line between Archie and Christina. They met, they lingered together for the least fraction of time, and that was enough. A charge as of electricity passed through Christina, and behold! the leaf of her psalm-book was torn across.

Archie was outside by the gate of the graveyard, conversing with Hob and the minister and shaking hands all round with the scattering congregation, when Clem and Christina were brought up to be presented.

The laird took off his hat and bowed to her with grace and respect.

Christina made her Glasgow curtsey to the laird, and went on again up the road for Hermiston and Cauldstaneslap, walking fast, breathing hurriedly with a heightened colour, and in this strange frame of mind, that when she was alone she seemed in high happiness, and when any one page 97 / 166

addressed her she resented it like a contradiction. A part of the way she had the company of some neighbour girls and a loutish young man; never had they seemed so insipid, never had she made herself so disagreeable. But these struck aside to their various destinations or were out-walked and left behind; and when she had driven off with sharp words the proffered convoy of some of her nephews and nieces, she was free to go on alone up Hermiston brae, walking on air, dwelling intoxicated among clouds of happiness. Near to the summit she heard steps behind her, a man's steps, light and very rapid. She knew the foot at once and walked the faster. "If it's me he's wanting, he can run for it," she thought, smiling.

Archie overtook her like a man whose mind was made up.

"Miss Kirstie," he began.

"Miss Christina, if you please, Mr. Weir," she interrupted. "I canna bear the contraction."

"You forget it has a friendly sound for me. Your aunt is an old friend of mine, and a very good one. I hope we shall see much of you at Hermiston?"

"My aunt and my sister-in-law doesna agree very well. Not that I have much ado with it. But still when I'm stopping in the house, if I was to page 98 / 166

be visiting my aunt, it would not look considerate-like."

"I am sorry," said Archie.

"I thank you kindly, Mr. Weir," she said. "I whiles think myself it's a great peety."

"Ah, I am sure your voice would always be for peace!" he cried.

"I wouldna be too sure of that," she said. "I have my days like other folk, I suppose."

"Do you know, in our old kirk, among our good old grey dames, you made an effect like sunshine."

"Ah, but that would be my Glasgow clothes!"

"I did not think I was so much under the influence of pretty frocks."

She smiled with a half look at him. "There's more than you!" she said.

"But you see I'm only Cinderella. I'll have to put all these things by in my trunk; next Sunday I'll be as grey as the rest. They're Glasgow clothes, you see, and it would never do to make a practice of it. It would seem terrible conspicuous."

By that they were come to the place where their ways severed. The old grey moors were all about them; in the midst a few sheep wandered; and they could see on the one hand the straggling caravan scaling the braes in front of them for Cauldstaneslap, and on the other, the contingent from Hermiston bending off and beginning to disappear by detachments into the policy gate. It was in these circumstances that they turned to say farewell, and deliberately exchanged a glance as they shook hands.

All passed as it should, genteelly; and in Christina's mind, as she mounted the first steep ascent for Cauldstaneslap, a gratifying sense of triumph prevailed over the recollection of minor lapses and mistakes.

She had kilted her gown, as she did usually at that rugged pass; but when she spied Archie still standing and gazing after her, the skirts came down again as if by enchantment. Here was a piece of nicety for that upland parish, where the matrons marched with their coats kilted in the rain, and the lasses walked barefoot to kirk through the dust of summer, and went bravely down by the burn-side, and sat on stones to make a public toilet before entering! It was perhaps an air wafted from Glasgow; or perhaps it marked a stage of that dizziness of gratified vanity, in which the instinctive act passed unperceived. He was looking after! She unloaded her bosom of a prodigious sigh that was all pleasure, and betook herself to run. When she had overtaken the stragglers of her family, she caught up the niece whom she had so recently repulsed, and kissed and slapped her, and drove her away again, and ran after her with pretty cries and laughter. Perhaps she thought the laird might still be looking! But it chanced the little scene came under the view of eyes less favourable; for she overtook Mrs. Hob page 100 / 166

marching with Clem and Dand.

"You're shurely fey, lass!" quoth Dandie.

"Think shame to yersel', miss!" said the strident Mrs. Hob. "Is this the gait to guide yersel' on the way hame frae kirk? You're shiirely no sponsible the day! And anyway I would mind my guid claes."

"Hoot!" said Christina, and went on before them head in air, treading the rough track with the tread of a wild doe.

She was in love with herself, her destiny, the air of the hills, the benediction of the sun. All the way home, she continued under the intoxication of these sky-scraping spirits. At table she could talk freely of young Hermiston; gave her opinion of him off-hand and with a loud voice, that he was a handsome young gentleman, real well mannered and sensible-like, but it was a pity he looked doleful. Only - the moment after - a memory of his eyes in church embarrassed her. But for this inconsiderable check, all through meal-time she had a good appetite, and she kept them laughing at table, until Gib (who had returned before them from Crossmichael and his separative worship) reproved the whole of them for their levity.

Singing "in to herself" as she went, her mind still in the turmoil of a glad confusion, she rose and tripped upstairs to a little loft, lighted page 101 / 166 by four panes in the gable, where she slept with one of her nieces. The niece, who followed her, presuming on "Auntie's" high spirits, was flounced out of the apartment with small ceremony, and retired, smarting and half tearful, to bury her woes in the byre among the hay. Still humming, Christina divested herself of her finery, and put her treasures one by one in her great green trunk. The last of these was the psalm-book; it was a fine piece, the gift of Mistress Clem, in distinct old-faced type, on paper that had begun to grow foxy in the warehouse - not by service -

and she was used to wrap it in a handkerchief every Sunday after its period of service was over, and bury it end-wise at the head of her trunk. As she now took it in hand the book fell open where the leaf was torn, and she stood and gazed upon that evidence of her bygone discomposure. There returned again the vision of the two brown eyes staring at her, intent and bright, out of that dark corner of the kirk.

The whole appearance and attitude, the smile, the suggested gesture of young Hermiston came before her in a flash at the sight of the torn page. "I was surely fey!" she said, echoing the words of Dandie, and at the suggested doom her high spirits deserted her. She flung herself prone upon the bed, and lay there, holding the psalm-book in her hands for hours, for the more part in a mere stupor of unconsenting pleasure and unreasoning fear. The fear was superstitious; there came up again and again in her memory Dandie's ill-omened words, and a hundred grisly and black tales out of the immediate neighbourhood read her a commentary on their force. The pleasure was never realised. You might say the joints of her body thought and remembered, and were gladdened, but her essential self, in the immediate theatre of consciousness, talked feverishly of something else, like a nervous person at a fire. The image that she most complacently dwelt on was that of Miss Christina

in her character of the Fair Lass of Cauldstaneslap, carrying all before her in the straw-coloured frock, the violet mantle, and the yellow cobweb stockings. Archie's image, on the other hand, when it presented itself was never welcomed - far less welcomed with any ardour, and it was exposed at times to merciless criticism. In the long vague dialogues she held in her mind, often with imaginary, often with unrealised interlocutors, Archie, if he were referred to at all came in for savage handling. He was described as "looking like a stork," "staring like a caulf," "a face like a ghaist's." "Do you call that manners?" she said; or, "I soon put him in his place." " `MISS CHRISTINA, IF YOU PLEASE, MR. WEIR!' says I, and just flyped up my skirt tails." With gabble like this she would entertain herself long whiles together, and then her eye would perhaps fall on the torn leaf, and the eyes of Archie would appear again from the darkness of the wall, and the voluble words deserted her, and she would lie still and stupid, and think upon nothing with devotion, and be sometimes raised by a quiet sigh. Had a doctor of medicine come into that loft, he would have diagnosed a healthy, well-developed, eminently vivacious lass lying on her face in a fit of the sulks; not one who had just contracted, or was just contracting, a mortal sickness of the mind which should yet carry her towards death and despair. Had it been a doctor of psychology, he might have been pardoned for divining in the girl a passion of childish vanity, self-love IN EXCELSIS, and no more.

It is to be understood that I have been painting chaos and describing the inarticulate. Every lineament that appears is too precise, almost every word used too strong. Take a finger-post in the mountains on a day of rolling mists; I have but copied the names that appear upon the pointers, the names of definite and famous cities far distant, and now perhaps basking in sunshine; but Christina remained all these hours, as page 103 / 166

it were, at the foot of the post itself, not moving, and enveloped in mutable and blinding wreaths of haze.

The day was growing late and the sunbeams long and level, when she sat suddenly up, and wrapped in its handkerchief and put by that psalm-book which had already played a part so decisive in the first chapter of her love-story. In the absence of the mesmerist's eye, we are told nowadays that the head of a bright nail may fill his place, if it be steadfastly regarded. So that torn page had riveted her attention on what might else have been but little, and perhaps soon forgotten; while the ominous words of Dandie - heard, not heeded, and still remembered - had lent to her thoughts, or rather to her mood, a cast of solemnity, and that idea of Fate - a pagan Fate, uncontrolled by any Christian deity, obscure, lawless, and august - moving indissuadably in the affairs of Christian men. Thus even that phenomenon of love at first sight, which is so rare and seems so simple and violent, like a disruption of life's tissue, may be decomposed into a sequence of accidents happily concurring.

She put on a grey frock and a pink kerchief, looked at herself a moment with approval in the small square of glass that served her for a toilet mirror, and went softly downstairs through the sleeping house that resounded with the sound of afternoon snoring. Just outside the door, Dandie was sitting with a book in his hand, not reading, only honouring the Sabbath by a sacred vacancy of mind. She came near him and stood still.

"I'm for off up the muirs, Dandie," she said.

There was something unusually soft in her tones that made him look up.

She was pale, her eyes dark and bright; no trace remained of the levity of the morning.

"Ay, lass? Ye'll have yer ups and downs like me, I'm thinkin'," he observed.

"What for do ye say that?" she asked.

"O, for naething," says Dand. "Only I think ye're mair like me than the lave of them. Ye've mair of the poetic temper, tho' Guid kens little enough of the poetic taalent. It's an ill gift at the best. Look at yoursel'. At denner you were all sunshine and flowers and laughter, and now you're like the star of evening on a lake."

She drank in this hackneyed compliment like wine, and it glowed in her veins.

"But I'm saying, Dand" - she came nearer him - "I'm for the muirs. I must have a braith of air. If Clem was to be speiring for me, try and quaiet him, will ye no?"

"What way?" said Dandie. "I ken but the ae way, and that's leein'."

I'll say ye had a sair heid, if ye like."

"But I havena," she objected.

"I daursay no," he returned. "I said I would say ye had; and if ye like to nay-say me when ye come back, it'll no mateerially maitter, for my chara'ter's clean gane a'ready past reca'."

"O, Dand, are ye a lecar?" she asked, lingering.

"Folks say sae," replied the bard.

"Wha says sae?" she pursued.

"Them that should ken the best," he responded. "The lassies, for ane."

"But, Dand, you would never lee to me?" she asked.

"I'll leave that for your pairt of it, ye girzie," said he. "Ye'll lee to me fast eneuch, when ye hae gotten a jo. I'm tellin' ye and it's true; when you have a jo, Miss Kirstie, it'll be for guid and ill. I ken: I was made that way mysel', but the deil was in my luck! Here, gang awa wi' ye to your muirs, and let me be; I'm in an hour of page 106 / 166

inspiraution, ye upsetting tawpie!"

But she clung to her brother's neighbourhood, she knew not why.

"Will ye no gie's a kiss, Dand?" she said. "I aye likit ye fine."

He kissed her and considered her a moment; he found something strange in her. But he was a libertine through and through, nourished equal contempt and suspicion of all womankind, and paid his way among them habitually with idle compliments.

"Gae wa' wi' ye!" said he. "Ye're a dentie baby, and be content wi' that!"

That was Dandie's way; a kiss and a comfit to Jenny - a bawbee and my blessing to Jill - and goodnight to the whole clan of ye, my dears!

When anything approached the serious, it became a matter for men, he both thought and said. Women, when they did not absorb, were only children to be shoo'd away. Merely in his character of connoisseur, however, Dandie glanced carelessly after his sister as she crossed the meadow. "The brat's no that bad!" he thought with surprise, for though he had just been paying her compliments, he had not really looked at her. "Hey! what's yon?" For the grey dress was cut with short sleeves and skirts, and displayed her trim strong legs clad in pink stockings of the same shade as the kerchief she wore round her shoulders, and that page 107 / 166

shimmered as she went. This was not her way in undress; he knew her ways and the ways of the whole sex in the country-side, no one better; when they did not go barefoot, they wore stout "rig and furrow" woollen hose of an invisible blue mostly, when they were not black outright; and Dandie, at sight of this daintiness, put two and two together. It was a silk handkerchief, then they would be silken hose; they matched - then the whole outfit was a present of Clem's, a costly present, and not something to be worn through bog and briar, or on a late afternoon of Sunday. He whistled. "My denty May, either your heid's fair turned, or there's some ongoings!" he observed, and dismissed the subject.

She went slowly at first, but ever straighter and faster for the Cauldstaneslap, a pass among the hills to which the farm owed its name.

The Slap opened like a doorway between two rounded hillocks; and through this ran the short cut to Hermiston. Immediately on the other side it went down through the Deil's Hags, a considerable marshy hollow of the hill tops, full of springs, and crouching junipers, and pools where the black peat-water slumbered. There was no view from here. A man might have sat upon the Praying Weaver's stone a half century, and seen none but the Cauldstaneslap children twice in the twenty-four hours on their way to the school and back again, an occasional shepherd, the irruption of a clan of sheep, or the birds who haunted about the springs, drinking and shrilly piping. So, when she had once passed the Slap, Kirstie was received into seclusion. She looked back a last time at the farm. It still lay deserted except for the figure of Dandie, who was now seen to be scribbling in his lap, the hour of expected inspiration having come to him at last. Thence she passed rapidly through the morass, and came page 108 / 166

to the farther end of it, where a sluggish burn discharges, and the path for Hermiston accompanies it on the beginning of its downward path.

From this corner a wide view was opened to her of the whole stretch of braes upon the other side, still sallow and in places rusty with the winter, with the path marked boldly, here and there by the burn-side a tuft of birches, and - two miles off as the crow flies - from its enclosures and young plantations, the windows of Hermiston glittering in the western sun.

Here she sat down and waited, and looked for a long time at these far-away bright panes of glass. It amused her to have so extended a view, she thought. It amused her to see the house of Hermiston - to see "folk"; and there was an indistinguishable human unit, perhaps the gardener, visibly sauntering on the gravel paths.

By the time the sun was down and all the easterly braes lay plunged in clear shadow, she was aware of another figure coming up the path at a most unequal rate of approach, now half running, now pausing and seeming to hesitate. She watched him at first with a total suspension of thought. She held her thought as a person holds his breathing. Then she consented to recognise him. "He'll no be coming here, he canna be; it's no possible." And there began to grow upon her a subdued choking suspense. He WAS coming; his hesitations had quite ceased, his step grew firm and swift; no doubt remained; and the question loomed up before her instant: what was she to do? It was all very well to say that her brother was a laird himself: it was all very well to speak of casual intermarriages and to count cousinship, like Auntie Kirstie. The page 109 / 166

difference in their social station was trenchant; propriety, prudence, all that she had ever learned, all that she knew, bade her flee. But on the other hand the cup of life now offered to her was too enchanting.

For one moment, she saw the question clearly, and definitely made her choice. She stood up and showed herself an instant in the gap relieved upon the sky line; and the next, fled trembling and sat down glowing with excitement on the Weaver's stone. She shut her eyes, seeking, praying for composure. Her hand shook in her lap, and her mind was full of incongruous and futile speeches. What was there to make a work about? She could take care of herself, she supposed! There was no harm in seeing the laird. It was the best thing that could happen. She would mark a proper distance to him once and for all. Gradually the wheels of her nature ceased to go round so madly, and she sat in passive expectation, a quiet, solitary figure in the midst of the grey moss. I have said she was no hypocrite, but here I am at fault. She never admitted to herself that she had come up the hill to look for Archie.

And perhaps after all she did not know, perhaps came as a stone falls.

For the steps of love in the young, and especially in girls, are instinctive and unconscious.

In the meantime Archie was drawing rapidly near, and he at least was consciously seeking her neighbourhood. The afternoon had turned to ashes in his mouth; the memory of the girl had kept him from reading and drawn him as with cords; and at last, as the cool of the evening began to come on, he had taken his hat and set forth, with a smothered ejaculation, by the moor path to Cauldstaneslap. He had no hope to find her; he took the off chance without expectation of result and to relieve page 110 / 166

his uneasiness. The greater was his surprise, as he surmounted the slope and came into the hollow of the Deil's Hags, to see there, like an answer to his wishes, the little womanly figure in the grey dress and the pink kerchief sitting little, and low, and lost, and acutely solitary, in these desolate surroundings and on the weather-beaten stone of the dead weaver. Those things that still smacked of winter were all rusty about her, and those things that already relished of the spring had put forth the tender and lively colours of the season. Even in the unchanging face of the death-stone, changes were to be remarked; and in the channeled lettering, the moss began to renew itself in jewels of green. By an afterthought that was a stroke of art, she had turned up over her head the back of the kerchief; so that it now framed becomingly her vivacious and yet pensive face. Her feet were gathered under her on the one side, and she leaned on her bare arm, which showed out strong and round, tapered to a slim wrist, and shimmered in the fading light.

Young Hermiston was struck with a certain chill. He was reminded that he now dealt in serious matters of life and death. This was a grown woman he was approaching, endowed with her mysterious potencies and attractions, the treasury of the continued race, and he was neither better nor worse than the average of his sex and age. He had a certain delicacy which had preserved him hitherto unspotted, and which (had either of them guessed it) made him a more dangerous companion when his heart should be really stirred. His throat was dry as he came near; but the appealing sweetness of her smile stood between them like a guardian angel.

page 111 / 166

For she turned to him and smiled, though without rising. There was a shade in this cavalier greeting that neither of them perceived; neither he, who simply thought it gracious and charming as herself; nor yet she, who did not observe (quick as she was) the difference between rising to meet the laird, and remaining seated to receive the expected admirer.

"Are ye stepping west, Hermiston?" said she, giving him his territorial name after the fashion of the country-side.

"I was," said he, a little hoarsely, "but I think I will be about the end of my stroll now. Are you like me, Miss Christina? The house would not hold me. I came here seeking air."

He took his seat at the other end of the tombstone and studied her, wondering what was she. There was infinite import in the question alike for her and him.

"Ay," she said. "I couldna bear the roof either. It's a habit of mine to come up here about the gloaming when it's quaiet and caller."

"It was a habit of my mother's also," he said gravely. The recollection half startled him as he expressed it. He looked around. "I have scarce been here since. It's peaceful," he said, with a long breath.

"It's no like Glasgow," she replied. "A weary place, yon Glasgow! But what a day have I had for my homecoming, and what a bonny evening!"

"Indeed, it was a wonderful day," said Archie. "I think I will remember it years and years until I come to die. On days like this - I do not know if you feel as I do - but everything appears so brief, and fragile, and exquisite, that I am afraid to touch life. We are here for so short a time; and all the old people before us - Rutherfords of Hermiston, Elliotts of the Cauldstaneslap - that were here but a while since riding about and keeping up a great noise in this quiet corner - making love too, and marrying - why, where are they now? It's deadly commonplace, but, after all, the commonplaces are the great poetic truths."

He was sounding her, semi-consciously, to see if she could understand him; to learn if she were only an animal the colour of flowers, or had a soul in her to keep her sweet. She, on her part, her means well in hand, watched, womanlike, for any opportunity to shine, to abound in his humour, whatever that might be. The dramatic artist, that lies dormant or only half awake in most human beings, had in her sprung to his feet in a divine fury, and chance had served her well. She looked upon him with a subdued twilight look that became the hour of the day and the train of thought; earnestness shone through her like stars in the purple west; and from the great but controlled upheaval of her whole nature there passed into her voice, and rang in her lightest words, a thrill of emotion.

"Have you mind of Dand's song?" she answered. "I think he'll have been trying to say what you have been thinking."

"No, I never heard it," he said. "Repeat it to me, can you?"

"It's nothing wanting the tune," said Kirstie.

"Then sing it me," said he.

"On the Lord's Day? That would never do, Mr. Weir!"

"I am afraid I am not so strict a keeper of the Sabbath, and there is no one in this place to hear us, unless the poor old ancient under the stone."

"No that I'm thinking that really," she said. "By my way of thinking, it's just as serious as a psalm. Will I sooth it to ye, then?"

"If you please," said he, and, drawing near to her on the tombstone, prepared to listen.

She sat up as if to sing. "I'll only can sooth it to ye," she explained.

"I wouldna like to sing out loud on the Sabbath. I think the birds would carry news of it to Gilbert," and she smiled. "It's about the page

Elliotts," she continued, "and I think there's few bonnier bits in the book-poets, though Dand has never got printed yet."

And she began, in the low, clear tones of her half voice, now sinking almost to a whisper, now rising to a particular note which was her best, and which Archie learned to wait for with growing emotion:-

"O they rade in the rain, in the days that are gane, In the rain and the wind and the lave,

They shoutit in the ha' and they routit on the hill, But they're a' quaitit noo in the grave.

Auld, auld Elliotts, clay-cauld Elliotts, dour, bauld Elliotte of auld!"

All the time she sang she looked steadfastly before her, her knees straight, her hands upon her knee, her head cast back and up. The expression was admirable throughout, for had she not learned it from the lips and under the criticism of the author? When it was done, she turned upon Archie a face softly bright, and eyes gently suffused and shining in the twilight, and his heart rose and went out to her with boundless pity and sympathy. His question was answered. She was a human being tuned to a sense of the tragedy of life; there were pathos and music and a great heart in the girl.

He arose instinctively, she also; for she saw she had gained a point, and scored the impression deeper, and she had wit enough left to flee upon a victory. They were but commonplaces that remained to be page 115 / 166

exchanged, but the low, moved voices in which they passed made them sacred in the memory. In the falling greyness of the evening he watched her figure winding through the morass, saw it turn a last time and wave a hand, and then pass through the Slap; and it seemed to him as if something went along with her out of the deepest of his heart. And something surely had come, and come to dwell there. He had retained from childhood a picture, now half obliterated by the passage of time and the multitude of fresh impressions, of his mother telling him, with the fluttered earnestness of her voice, and often with dropping tears, the tale of the "Praying Weaver," on the very scene of his brief tragedy and long repose. And now there was a companion piece; and he beheld, and he should behold for ever, Christina perched on the same tomb, in the grey colours of the evening, gracious, dainty, perfect as a flower, and she also singing-

"Of old, unhappy far off things,

And battles long ago,"

of their common ancestors now dead, of their rude wars composed, their weapons buried with them, and of these strange changelings, their descendants, who lingered a little in their places, and would soon be gone also, and perhaps sung of by others at the gloaming hour. By one of the unconscious arts of tenderness the two women were enshrined together in his memory. Tears, in that hour of sensibility, came into his eyes indifferently at the thought of either; and the girl, from being something merely bright and shapely, was caught up into the zone of things serious as life and death and his dead mother. So that in all page 116 / 166 ways and on either side, Fate played his game artfully with this poor pair of children. The generations were prepared, the pangs were made ready, before the curtain rose on the dark drama.

In the same moment of time that she disappeared from Archie, there opened before Kirstie's eyes the cup-like hollow in which the farm lay.

She saw, some five hundred feet below her, the house making itself bright with candles, and this was a broad hint to her to hurry. For they were only kindled on a Sabbath night with a view to that family worship which rounded in the incomparable tedium of the day and brought on the relaxation of supper. Already she knew that Robert must be within-sides at the head of the table, "waling the portions"; for it was Robert in his quality of family priest and judge, not the gifted Gilbert, who officiated. She made good time accordingly down the steep ascent, and came up to the door panting as the three younger brothers, all roused at last from slumber, stood together in the cool and the dark of the evening with a fry of nephews and nieces about them, chatting and awaiting the expected signal. She stood back; she had no mind to direct attention to her late arrival or to her labouring breath.

"Kirstie, ye have shaved it this time, my lass?" said Clem. "Whaur were ye?"

"O, just taking a dander by mysel'," said Kirstie.

And the talk continued on the subject of the American War, without page 117 / 166

further reference to the truant who stood by them in the covert of the dusk, thrilling with happiness and the sense of guilt.

The signal was given, and the brothers began to go in one after another, amid the jostle and throng of Hob's children.

Only Dandie, waiting till the last, caught Kirstie by the arm. "When did ye begin to dander in pink hosen, Mistress Elliott?" he whispered slyly.

She looked down; she was one blush. "I maun have forgotten to change them," said she; and went into prayers in her turn with a troubled mind, between anxiety as to whether Dand should have observed her yellow stockings at church, and should thus detect her in a palpable falsehood, and shame that she had already made good his prophecy. She remembered the words of it, how it was to be when she had gotten a jo, and that that would be for good and evil. "Will I have gotten my jo now?" she thought with a secret rapture.

And all through prayers, where it was her principal business to conceal the pink stockings from the eyes of the indifferent Mrs. Hob - and all through supper, as she made a feint of eating and sat at the table radiant and constrained - and again when she had left them and come into her chamber, and was alone with her sleeping niece, and could at last lay aside the armour of society - the same words sounded within her, the same profound note of happiness, of a world all changed and renewed, of page 118 / 166

a day that had been passed in Paradise, and of a night that was to be heaven opened. All night she seemed to be conveyed smoothly upon a shallow stream of sleep and waking, and through the bowers of Beulah; all night she cherished to her heart that exquisite hope; and if, towards morning, she forgot it a while in a more profound unconsciousness, it was to catch again the rainbow thought with her first moment of awaking.

CHAPTER VII - ENTER MEPHISTOPHELES

TWO days later a gig from Crossmichael deposited Frank Innes at the doors of Hermiston. Once in a way, during the past winter, Archie, in some acute phase of boredom, had written him a letter. It had contained something in the nature of an invitation or a reference to an invitation

- precisely what, neither of them now remembered. When Innes had received it, there had been nothing further from his mind than to bury himself in the moors with Archie; but not even the most acute political heads are guided through the steps of life with unerring directness.

That would require a gift of prophecy which has been denied to man. For instance, who could have imagined that, not a month after he had received the letter, and turned it into mockery, and put off answering it, and in the end lost it, misfortunes of a gloomy cast should begin to thicken over Frank's career? His case may be briefly stated. His father, a small Morayshire laird with a large family, became recalcitrant and cut off the supplies; he had fitted himself out with the beginnings of quite a good law library, which, upon some sudden losses on the turf, he had been obliged to sell before they were paid page 119 / 166

for; and his bookseller, hearing some rumour of the event, took out a warrant for his arrest. Innes had early word of it, and was able to take precautions. In this immediate welter of his affairs, with an unpleasant charge hanging over him, he had judged it the part of prudence to be off instantly, had written a fervid letter to his father at Inverauld, and put himself in the coach for Crossmichael. Any port in a storm!

He was manfully turning his back on the Parliament House and its gay babble, on porter and oysters, the race-course and the ring; and manfully prepared, until these clouds should have blown by, to share a living grave with Archie Weir at Hermiston.

To do him justice, he was no less surprised to be going than Archie was to see him come; and he carried off his wonder with an infinitely better grace.

"Well, here I am!" said he, as he alighted. "Pylades has come to Orestes at last. By the way, did you get my answer? No? How very provoking! Well, here I am to answer for myself, and that's better still."

"I am very glad to see you, of course," said Archie. "I make you heartily welcome, of course. But you surely have not come to stay, with the Courts still sitting; is that not most unwise?"

"Damn the Courts!" says Frank. "What are the Courts to friendship and a little fishing?"

page 120 / 166

And so it was agreed that he was to stay, with no term to the visit but the term which he had privily set to it himself - the day, namely, when his father should have come down with the dust, and he should be able to pacify the bookseller. On such vague conditions there began for these two young men (who were not even friends) a life of great familiarity and, as the days drew on, less and less intimacy. They were together at meal times, together o' nights when the hour had come for whisky-toddy; but it might have been noticed (had there been any one to pay heed) that they were rarely so much together by day. Archie had Hermiston to attend to, multifarious activities in the hills, in which he did not require, and had even refused, Frank's escort. He would be off sometimes in the morning and leave only a note on the breakfast table to announce the fact; and sometimes, with no notice at all, he would not return for dinner until the hour was long past. Innes groaned under these desertions; it required all his philosophy to sit down to a solitary breakfast with composure, and all his unaffected good-nature to be able to greet Archie with friendliness on the more rare occasions when he came home late for dinner.

"I wonder what on earth he finds to do, Mrs. Elliott?" said he one morning, after he had just read the hasty billet and sat down to table.

"I suppose it will be business, sir," replied the housekeeper drily, measuring his distance off to him by an indicated curtsy.

page 121 / 166

"But I can't imagine what business!" he reiterated.

"I suppose it will be HIS business," retorted the austere Kirstie.

He turned to her with that happy brightness that made the charm of his disposition, and broke into a peal of healthy and natural laughter.

"Well played, Mrs. Elliott!" he cried; and the housekeeper's face relaxed into the shadow of an iron smile. "Well played indeed!" said he. "But you must not be making a stranger of me like that. Why, Archie and I were at the High School together, and we've been to college together, and we were going to the Bar together, when - you know! Dear, dear me! what a pity that was! A life spoiled, a fine young fellow as good as buried here in the wilderness with rustics; and all for what? A frolic, silly, if you like, but no more. God, how good your scones are, Mrs. Elliott!"

"They're no mines, it was the lassie made them," said Kirstie; "and, saving your presence, there's little sense in taking the Lord's name in vain about idle vivers that you fill your kyte wi'."

"I daresay you're perfectly right, ma'am," quoth the imperturbable Frank. "But as I was saying, this is a pitiable business, this about poor Archie; and you and I might do worse than put our heads together, like a couple of sensible people, and bring it to an end. Let me tell page 122 / 166

you, ma'am, that Archie is really quite a promising young man, and in my opinion he would do well at the Bar. As for his father, no one can deny his ability, and I don't fancy any one would care to deny that he has the deil's own temper - "

"If you'll excuse me, Mr. Innes, I think the lass is crying on me," said Kirstie, and flounced from the room.

"The damned, cross-grained, old broomstick!" ejaculated Innes.

In the meantime, Kirstie had escaped into the kitchen, and before her vassal gave vent to her feelings.

"Here, ettercap! Ye'll have to wait on yon Innes! I canna haud myself in. `Puir Erchie!' I'd `puir Erchie' him, if I had my way! And Hermiston with the deil's ain temper! God, let him take Hermiston's scones out of his mouth first. There's no a hair on ayther o' the Weirs that hasna mair spunk and dirdum to it than what he has in his hale dwaibly body! Settin' up his snash to me! Let him gang to the black toon where he's mebbe wantit - birling in a curricle - wi' pimatum on his heid - making a mess o' himsel' wi' nesty hizzies - a fair disgrace!" It was impossible to hear without admiration Kirstie's graduated disgust, as she brought forth, one after another, these somewhat baseless charges. Then she remembered her immediate purpose, and turned again on her fascinated auditor. "Do ye no hear me, tawpie?

Do ye no hear what I'm tellin' ye? Will I have to shoo ye in to him?

page 123 / 166

If I come to attend to ye, mistress!" And the maid fled the kitchen, which had become practically dangerous, to attend on Innes' wants in the front parlour.

TANTAENE IRAE? Has the reader perceived the reason? Since Frank's coming there were no more hours of gossip over the supper tray! All his blandishments were in vain; he had started handicapped on the race for Mrs. Elliott's favour.

But it was a strange thing how misfortune dogged him in his efforts to be genial. I must guard the reader against accepting Kirstie's epithets as evidence; she was more concerned for their vigour than for their accuracy. Dwaibly, for instance; nothing could be more calumnious.

Frank was the very picture of good looks, good humour, and manly youth.

He had bright eyes with a sparkle and a dance to them, curly hair, a charming smile, brilliant teeth, an admirable carriage of the head, the look of a gentleman, the address of one accustomed to please at first sight and to improve the impression. And with all these advantages, he failed with every one about Hermiston; with the silent shepherd, with the obsequious grieve, with the groom who was also the ploughman, with the gardener and the gardener's sister - a pious, down-hearted woman with a shawl over her ears - he failed equally and flatly. They did not like him, and they showed it. The little maid, indeed, was an exception; she admired him devoutly, probably dreamed of him in her private hours; but she was accustomed to play the part of silent auditor to Kirstie's tirades and silent recipient of Kirstie's buffets, and she had learned not only to be a very capable girl of her years, but a very page 124 / 166

secret and prudent one besides. Frank was thus conscious that he had one ally and sympathiser in the midst of that general union of disfavour that surrounded, watched, and waited on him in the house of Hermiston; but he had little comfort or society from that alliance, and the demure little maid (twelve on her last birthday) preserved her own counsel, and tripped on his service, brisk, dumbly responsive, but inexorably unconversational. For the others, they were beyond hope and beyond endurance. Never had a young Apollo been cast among such rustic barbarians. But perhaps the cause of his ill-success lay in one trait which was habitual and unconscious with him, yet diagnostic of the man.

It was his practice to approach any one person at the expense of some one else. He offered you an alliance against the some one else; he flattered you by slighting him; you were drawn into a small intrigue against him before you knew how. Wonderful are the virtues of this process generally; but Frank's mistake was in the choice of the some one else. He was not politic in that; he listened to the voice of irritation. Archie had offended him at first by what he had felt to be rather a dry reception, had offended him since by his frequent absences.

He was besides the one figure continually present in Frank's eye; and it was to his immediate dependants that Frank could offer the snare of his sympathy. Now the truth is that the Weirs, father and son, were surrounded by a posse of strenuous loyalists. Of my lord they were vastly proud. It was a distinction in itself to be one of the vassals of the "Hanging Judge," and his gross, formidable joviality was far from unpopular in the neighbourhood of his home. For Archie they had, one and all, a sensitive affection and respect which recoiled from a word of belittlement.

Nor was Frank more successful when he went farther afield. To the Four Black Brothers, for instance, he was antipathetic in the highest degree.

Hob thought him too light, Gib too profane. Clem, who saw him but for a day or two before he went to Glasgow, wanted to know what the fule's business was, and whether he meant to stay here all session time!

"Yon's a drone," he pronounced. As for Dand, it will be enough to describe their first meeting, when Frank had been whipping a river and the rustic celebrity chanced to come along the path.

"I'm told you're quite a poet," Frank had said.

"Wha tell't ye that, mannie?" had been the unconciliating answer.

"O, everybody!" says Frank.

"God! Here's fame!" said the sardonic poet, and he had passed on his way.

Come to think of it, we have here perhaps a truer explanation of Frank's failures. Had he met Mr. Sheriff Scott he could have turned a neater compliment, because Mr. Scott would have been a friend worth making.

Dand, on the other hand, he did not value sixpence, and he showed it even while he tried to flatter. Condescension is an excellent thing, but it is strange how one-sided the pleasure of it is! He who goes page 126 / 166

fishing among the Scots peasantry with condescension for a bait will have an empty basket by evening.

In proof of this theory Frank made a great success of it at the Crossmichael Club, to which Archie took him immediately on his arrival; his own last appearance on that scene of gaiety. Frank was made welcome there at once, continued to go regularly, and had attended a meeting (as the members ever after loved to tell) on the evening before his death.

Young Hay and young Pringle appeared again. There was another supper at Windiclaws, another dinner at Driffel; and it resulted in Frank being taken to the bosom of the county people as unreservedly as he had been repudiated by the country folk. He occupied Hermiston after the manner of an invader in a conquered capital. He was perpetually issuing from it, as from a base, to toddy parties, fishing parties, and dinner parties, to which Archie was not invited, or to which Archie would not go. It was now that the name of The Recluse became general for the young man. Some say that Innes invented it; Innes, at least, spread it abroad.

"How's all with your Recluse to-day?" people would ask.

"O, reclusing away!" Innes would declare, with his bright air of saying something witty; and immediately interrupt the general laughter which he had provoked much more by his air than his words, "Mind you, it's all very well laughing, but I'm not very well pleased. Poor Archie is a good fellow, an excellent fellow, a fellow I always liked. I think it page 127 / 166

small of him to take his little disgrace so hard, and shut himself up.

'Grant that it is a ridiculous story, painfully ridiculous,' I keep telling him. 'Be a man! Live it down, man!' But not he. Of course, it's just solitude, and shame, and all that. But I confess I'm beginning to fear the result. It would be all the pities in the world if a really promising fellow like Weir was to end ill. I'm seriously tempted to write to Lord Hermiston, and put it plainly to him."

"I would if I were you," some of his auditors would say, shaking the head, sitting bewildered and confused at this new view of the matter, so deftly indicated by a single word. "A capital idea!" they would add, and wonder at the APLOMB and position of this young man, who talked as a matter of course of writing to Hermiston and correcting him upon his private affairs.

And Frank would proceed, sweetly confidential: "I'll give you an idea, now. He's actually sore about the way that I'm received and he's left out in the county - actually jealous and sore. I've rallied him and I've reasoned with him, told him that every one was most kindly inclined towards him, told him even that I was received merely because I was his guest. But it's no use. He will neither accept the invitations he gets, nor stop brooding about the ones where he's left out. What I'm afraid of is that the wound's ulcerating. He had always one of those dark, secret, angry natures - a little underhand and plenty of bile -

you know the sort. He must have inherited it from the Weirs, whom I suspect to have been a worthy family of weavers somewhere; what's the cant phrase? - sedentary occupation. It's precisely the kind of page 128 / 166

character to go wrong in a false position like what his father's made for him, or he's making for himself, whichever you like to call it. And for my part, I think it a disgrace," Frank would say generously.

Presently the sorrow and anxiety of this disinterested friend took shape. He began in private, in conversations of two, to talk vaguely of bad habits and low habits. "I must say I'm afraid he's going wrong altogether," he would say. "I'll tell you plainly, and between ourselves, I scarcely like to stay there any longer; only, man, I'm positively afraid to leave him alone. You'll see, I shall be blamed for it later on. I'm staying at a great sacrifice. I'm hindering my chances at the Bar, and I can't blind my eyes to it. And what I'm afraid of is that I'm going to get kicked for it all round before all's done. You see, nobody believes in friendship nowadays."

"Well, Innes," his interlocutor would reply, "it's very good of you, I must say that. If there's any blame going, you'll always be sure of MY

good word, for one thing."

"Well," Frank would continue, "candidly, I don't say it's pleasant. He has a very rough way with him; his father's son, you know. I don't say he's rude - of course, I couldn't be expected to stand that - but he steers very near the wind. No, it's not pleasant; but I tell ye, man, in conscience I don't think it would be fair to leave him. Mind you, I don't say there's anything actually wrong. What I say is that I don't like the looks of it, man!" and he would press the arm of his momentary

confidant.

In the early stages I am persuaded there was no malice. He talked but for the pleasure of airing himself. He was essentially glib, as becomes the young advocate, and essentially careless of the truth, which is the mark of the young ass; and so he talked at random. There was no particular bias, but that one which is indigenous and universal, to flatter himself and to please and interest the present friend. And by thus milling air out of his mouth, he had presently built up a presentation of Archie which was known and talked of in all corners of the county. Wherever there was a residential house and a walled garden, wherever there was a dwarfish castle and a park, wherever a quadruple cottage by the ruins of a peel-tower showed an old family going down, and wherever a handsome villa with a carriage approach and a shrubbery marked the coming up of a new one - probably on the wheels of machinery

- Archie began to be regarded in the light of a dark, perhaps a vicious mystery, and the future developments of his career to be looked for with uneasiness and confidential whispering. He had done something disgraceful, my dear. What, was not precisely known, and that good kind young man, Mr. Innes, did his best to make light of it. But there it was. And Mr. Innes was very anxious about him now; he was really uneasy, my dear; he was positively wrecking his own prospects because he dared not leave him alone. How wholly we all lie at the mercy of a single prater, not needfully with any malign purpose! And if a man but talks of himself in the right spirit, refers to his virtuous actions by the way, and never applies to them the name of virtue, how easily his evidence is accepted in the court of public opinion!

page 130 / 166

All this while, however, there was a more poisonous ferment at work between the two lads, which came late indeed to the surface, but had modified and magnified their dissensions from the first. To an idle, shallow, easy-going customer like Frank, the smell of a mystery was attractive. It gave his mind something to play with, like a new toy to a child; and it took him on the weak side, for like many young men coming to the Bar, and before they had been tried and found wanting, he flattered himself he was a fellow of unusual quickness and penetration.

They knew nothing of Sherlock Holmes in those days, but there was a good deal said of Talleyrand. And if you could have caught Frank off his guard, he would have confessed with a smirk that, if he resembled any one, it was the Marquis de Talleyrand-Perigord. It was on the occasion of Archie's first absence that this interest took root. It was vastly deepened when Kirstie resented his curiosity at breakfast, and that same afternoon there occurred another scene which clinched the business. He was fishing Swingleburn, Archie accompanying him, when the latter looked at his watch.

"Well, good-bye," said he. "I have something to do. See you at dinner."

"Don't be in such a hurry," cries Frank. "Hold on till I get my rod up.

I'll go with you; I'm sick of flogging this ditch."

And he began to reel up his line.

page 131 / 166

Archie stood speechless. He took a long while to recover his wits under this direct attack; but by the time he was ready with his answer, and the angle was almost packed up, he had become completely Weir, and the hanging face gloomed on his young shoulders. He spoke with a laboured composure, a laboured kindness even; but a child could see that his mind was made up.

"I beg your pardon, Innes; I don't want to be disagreeable, but let us understand one another from the beginning. When I want your company, I'll let you know."

"O!" cries Frank, "you don't want my company, don't you?"

"Apparently not just now," replied Archie. "I even indicated to you when I did, if you'll remember - and that was at dinner. If we two fellows are to live together pleasantly - and I see no reason why we should not - it can only be by respecting each other's privacy. If we begin intruding - "

"O, come! I'll take this at no man's hands. Is this the way you treat a guest and an old friend?" cried Innes.

"Just go home and think over what I said by yourself," continued Archie,

"whether it's reasonable, or whether it's really offensive or not; and page 132 / 166

let's meet at dinner as though nothing had happened, I'll put it this way, if you like - that I know my own character, that

I'm looking forward (with great pleasure, I assure you) to a long visit from you, and that I'm taking precautions at the first. I see the thing that we -

that I, if you like - might fall out upon, and I step in and OBSTO

PRINCIPIIS. I wager you five pounds you'll end by seeing that I mean friendliness, and I assure you, Francie, I do," he added, relenting.

Bursting with anger, but incapable of speech, Innes shouldered his rod, made a gesture of farewell, and strode off down the burn-side. Archie watched him go without moving. He was sorry, but quite unashamed. He hated to be inhospitable, but in one thing he was his father's son. He had a strong sense that his house was his own and no man else's; and to lie at a guest's mercy was what he refused. He hated to seem harsh.

But that was Frank's lookout. If Frank had been commonly discreet, he would have been decently courteous. And there was another consideration. The secret he was protecting was not his own merely; it was hers: it belonged to that inexpressible she who was fast taking possession of his soul, and whom he would soon have defended at the cost of burning cities. By the time he had watched Frank as far as the Swingleburn-foot, appearing and disappearing in the tarnished heather, still stalking at a fierce gait but already dwindled in the distance into less than the smallness of Lilliput, he could afford to smile at the occurrence. Either Frank would go, and that would be a relief - or he would continue to stay, and his host must continue to endure him.

And Archie was now free - by devious paths, behind hillocks and in the hollow of burns - to make for the trysting-place where Kirstie, cried page 133 / 166 about by the curlew and the plover, waited and burned for his coming by the Covenanter's stone.

Innes went off down-hill in a passion of resentment, easy to be understood, but which yielded progressively to the needs of his situation. He cursed Archie for a cold-hearted, unfriendly, rude, rude dog; and himself still more passionately for a fool in having come to Hermiston when he might have sought refuge in almost any other house in Scotland. But the step once taken, was practically irretrievable. He had no more ready money to go anywhere else; he would have to borrow from Archie the next club-night; and ill as he thought of his host's manners, he was sure of his practical generosity. Frank's resemblance to Talleyrand strikes me as imaginary; but at least not Talleyrand himself could have more obediently taken his lesson from the facts. He met Archie at dinner without resentment, almost with cordiality. You must take your friends as you find them, he would have said. Archie couldn't help being his father's son, or his grandfather's, the hypothetical weaver's, grandson. The son of a hunks, he was still a hunks at heart, incapable of true generosity and consideration; but he had other qualities with which Frank could divert himself in the meanwhile, and to enjoy which it was necessary that Frank should keep his temper.

So excellently was it controlled that he awoke next morning with his head full of a different, though a cognate subject. What was Archie's little game? Why did he shun Frank's company? What was he keeping secret? Was he keeping tryst with somebody, and was it a woman? It page 134 / 166

would be a good joke and a fair revenge to discover. To that task he set himself with a great deal of patience, which might have surprised his friends, for he had been always credited not with patience so much as brilliancy; and little by little, from one point to another, he at last succeeded in piecing out the situation. First he remarked that, although Archie set out in all the directions of the compass, he always came home again from some point between the south and west. From the study of a map, and in consideration of the great expanse of untenanted moorland running in that direction towards the sources of the Clyde, he laid his finger on Cauldstaneslap and two other neighbouring farms, Kingsmuirs and Polintarf. But it was difficult to advance farther.

With his rod for a pretext, he vainly visited each of them in turn; nothing was to be seen suspicious about this trinity of moorland settlements. He would have tried to follow Archie, had it been the least possible, but the nature of the land precluded the idea. He did the next best, ensconced himself in a quiet corner, and pursued his movements with a telescope. It was equally in vain, and he soon wearied of his futile vigilance, left the telescope at home, and had almost given the matter up in despair, when, on the twenty-seventh day of his visit, he was suddenly confronted with the person whom he sought. The first Sunday Kirstie had managed to stay away from kirk on some pretext of indisposition, which was more truly modesty; the pleasure of beholding Archie seeming too sacred, too vivid for that public place.

On the two following, Frank had himself been absent on some of his excursions among the neighbouring families. It was not until the fourth, accordingly, that Frank had occasion to set eyes on the enchantress. With the first look, all hesitation was over. She came with the Cauldstaneslap party; then she lived at Cauldstaneslap. Here page 135 / 166 was Archie's secret, here was the woman, and more than that - though I have need here of every manageable attenuation of language - with the first look, he had already entered himself as rival. It was a good deal in pique, it was a little in revenge, it was much in genuine admiration: the devil may decide the proportions! I cannot, and it is very likely that Frank could not.

"Mighty attractive milkmaid," he observed, on the way home.

"Who?" said Archie.

"O, the girl you're looking at - aren't you? Forward there on the road.

She came attended by the rustic bard; presumably, therefore, belongs to his exalted family. The single objection! for the four black brothers are awkward customers. If anything were to go wrong, Gib would gibber, and Clem would prove inclement; and Dand fly in danders, and Hob blow up in gobbets. It would be a Helliott of a business!"

"Very humorous, I am sure," said Archie.

"Well, I am trying to be so," said Frank. "It's none too easy in this place, and with your solemn society, my dear fellow. But confess that the milkmaid has found favour in your eyes, or resign all claim to be a man of taste."

page 136 / 166

"It is no matter," returned Archie.

But the other continued to look at him, steadily and quizzically, and his colour slowly rose and deepened under the glance, until not impudence itself could have denied that he was blushing. And at this Archie lost some of his control. He changed his stick from one hand to the other, and - "O, for God's sake, don't be an ass!" he cried.

"Ass? That's the retort delicate without doubt," says Frank. "Beware of the homespun brothers, dear. If they come into the dance, you'll see who's an ass. Think now, if they only applied (say) a quarter as much talent as I have applied to the question of what Mr. Archie does with his evening hours, and why he is so unaffectedly nasty when the subject's touched on - "

"You are touching on it now," interrupted Archie with a wince.

"Thank you. That was all I wanted, an articulate confession," said Frank.

"I beg to remind you - " began Archie.

But he was interrupted in turn. "My dear fellow, don't. It's quite needless. The subject's dead and buried."

page 137 / 166

And Frank began to talk hastily on other matters, an art in which he was an adept, for it was his gift to be fluent on anything or nothing. But although Archie had the grace or the timidity to suffer him to rattle on, he was by no means done with the subject. When he came home to dinner, he was greeted with a sly demand, how things were looking

"Cauldstaneslap ways." Frank took his first glass of port out after dinner to the toast of Kirstie, and later in the evening he returned to the charge again.

"I say, Weir, you'll excuse me for returning again to this affair. I've been thinking it over, and I wish to beg you very seriously to be more careful. It's not a safe business. Not safe, my boy," said he.

"What?" said Archie.

"Well, it's your own fault if I must put a name on the thing; but really, as a friend, I cannot stand by and see you rushing head down into these dangers. My dear boy," said he, holding up a warning cigar,

"consider! What is to be the end of it?"

"The end of what?" - Archie, helpless with irritation, persisted in this dangerous and ungracious guard.

"Well, the end of the milkmaid; or, to speak more by the card, the end page 138 / 166

of Miss Christina Elliott of the Cauldstaneslap."

"I assure you," Archie broke out, "this is all a figment of your imagination. There is nothing to be said against that young lady; you have no right to introduce her name into the conversation."

"I'll make a note of it," said Frank. "She shall henceforth be nameless, nameless, nameless, Grigalach! I make a note besides of your valuable testimony to her character. I only want to look at this thing as a man of the world. Admitted she's an angel - but, my good fellow, is she a lady?"

This was torture to Archie. "I beg your pardon," he said, struggling to be composed, "but because you have wormed yourself into my confidence - "

"O, come!" cried Frank. "Your confidence? It was rosy but unconsenting. Your confidence, indeed? Now, look! This is what I must say, Weir, for it concerns your safety and good character, and therefore my honour as your friend. You say I wormed myself into your confidence.

Wormed is good. But what have I done? I have put two and two together, just as the parish will be doing tomorrow, and the whole of Tweeddale in two weeks, and the black brothers - well, I won't put a date on that; it will be a dark and stormy morning! Your secret, in other words, is poor Poll's. And I want to ask of you as a friend whether you like the prospect? There are two horns to your dilemma, and I must say for myself I should look mighty ruefully on either. Do you see yourself page 139 / 166

explaining to the four Black Brothers? or do you see yourself presenting the milkmaid to papa as the future lady of Hermiston? Do you? I tell you plainly, I don't!"

Archie rose. "I will hear no more of this," he said, in a trembling voice.

But Frank again held up his cigar. "Tell me one thing first. Tell me if this is not a friend's part that I am playing?"

"I believe you think it so," replied Archle. "I can go as far as that.

I can do so much justice to your motives. But I will hear no more of it. I am going to bed."

"That's right, Weir," said Frank heartily. "Go to bed and think over it; and I say, man, don't forget your prayers! I don't often do the moral - don't go in for that sort of thing - but when I do there's one thing sure, that I mean it."

So Archie marched off to bed, and Frank sat alone by the table for another hour or so, smiling to himself richly. There was nothing vindictive in his nature; but, if revenge came in his way, it might as well be good, and the thought of Archie's pillow reflections that night was indescribably sweet to him. He felt a pleasant sense of power. He looked down on Archie as on a very little boy whose strings he pulled -

page 140 / 166

as on a horse whom he had backed and bridled by sheer power of intelligence, and whom he might ride to glory or the grave at pleasure.

Which was it to be? He lingered long, relishing the details of schemes that he was too idle to pursue. Poor cork upon a torrent, he tasted that night the sweets of omnipotence, and brooded like a deity over the strands of that intrigue which was to shatter him before the summer waned.

CHAPTER VIII - A NOCTURNAL VISIT

KIRSTIE had many causes of distress. More and more as we grow old - and yet more and more as we grow old and are women, frozen by the fear of age - we come to rely on the voice as the single outlet of the soul.

Only thus, in the curtailment of our means, can we relieve the straitened cry of the passion within us; only thus, in the bitter and sensitive shyness of advancing years, can we maintain relations with those vivacious figures of the young that still show before us and tend daily to become no more than the moving wall-paper of life. Talk is the last link, the last relation. But with the end of the conversation, when the voice stops and the bright face of the listener is turned away, solitude falls again on the bruised heart. Kirstie had lost her "cannie hour at e'en"; she could no more wander with Archie, a ghost if you will, but a happy ghost, in fields Elysian. And to her it was as if the whole world had fallen silent; to him, but an unremarkable change of amusements. And she raged to know it. The effervescency of her passionate and irritable nature rose within her at times to bursting point.

This is the price paid by age for unseasonable ardours of feeling. It must have been so for Kirstie at any time when the occasion chanced; but it so fell out that she was deprived of this delight in the hour when she had most need of it, when she had most to say, most to ask, and when she trembled to recognise her sovereignty not merely in abeyance but annulled. For, with the clairvoyance of a genuine love, she had pierced the mystery that had so long embarrassed Frank. She was conscious, even before it was carried out, even on that Sunday night when it began, of an invasion of her rights; and a voice told her the invader's name.

Since then, by arts, by accident, by small things observed, and by the general drift of Archie's humour, she had passed beyond all possibility of doubt. With a sense of justice that Lord Hermiston might have envied, she had that day in church considered and admitted the attractions of the younger Kirstie; and with the profound humanity and sentimentality of her nature, she had recognised the coming of fate.

Not thus would she have chosen. She had seen, in imagination, Archie wedded to some tall, powerful, and rosy heroine of the golden locks, made in her own image, for whom she would have strewed the bride-bed with delight; and now she could have wept to see the ambition falsified.

But the gods had pronounced, and her doom was otherwise.

She lay tossing in bed that night, besieged with feverish thoughts.

There were dangerous matters pending, a battle was toward, over the fate of which she hung in jealousy, sympathy, fear, and alternate loyalty and disloyalty to either side. Now she was reincarnated in her niece, and now in Archie. Now she saw, through the girl's eyes, the youth on his page 142 / 166

knees to her, heard his persuasive instances with a deadly weakness, and received his overmastering caresses. Anon, with a revulsion, her temper raged to see such utmost favours of fortune and love squandered on a brat of a girl, one of her own house, using her own name - a deadly ingredient - and that "didna ken her ain mind an' was as black's your hat." Now she trembled lest her deity should plead in vain, loving the idea of success for him like a triumph of nature; anon, with returning loyalty to her own family and sex, she trembled for Kirstie and the credit of the Elliotts. And again she had a vision of herself, the day over for her old-world tales and local gossip, bidding farewell to her last link with life and brightness and love; and behind and beyond, she saw but the blank butt-end where she must crawl to die. Had she then come to the lees? she, so great, so beautiful, with a heart as fresh as a girl's and strong as womanhood? It could not be, and yet it was so; and for a moment her bed was horrible to her as the sides of the grave.

And she looked forward over a waste of hours, and saw herself go on to rage, and tremble, and be softened, and rage again, until the day came and the labours of the day must be renewed.

Suddenly she heard feet on the stairs - his feet, and soon after the sound of a window-sash flung open. She sat up with her heart beating.

He had gone to his room alone, and he had not gone to bed. She might again have one of her night cracks; and at the entrancing prospect, a change came over her mind; with the approach of this hope of pleasure, all the baser metal became immediately obliterated from her thoughts.

She rose, all woman, and all the best of woman, tender, pitiful, hating the wrong, loyal to her own sex - and all the weakest of that dear page 143 / 166 miscellany, nourishing, cherishing next her soft heart, voicelessly flattering, hopes that she would have died sooner than have acknowledged. She tore off her nightcap, and her hair fell about her shoulders in profusion. Undying coquetry awoke. By the faint light of her nocturnal rush, she stood before the looking-glass, carried her shapely arms above her head, and gathered up the treasures of her tresses. She was never backward to admire herself; that kind of modesty was a stranger to her nature; and she paused, struck with a pleased wonder at the sight. "Ye daft auld wife!" she said, answering a thought that was not; and she blushed with the innocent consciousness of a child. Hastily she did up the massive and shining coils, hastily donned a wrapper, and with the rushlight in her hand, stole into the hall.

Below stairs she heard the clock ticking the deliberate seconds, and Frank jingling with the decanters in the dining-room. Aversion rose in her, bitter and momentary. "Nesty, tippling puggy!" she thought; and the next moment she had knocked guardedly at Archie's door and was bidden enter.

Archie had been looking out into the ancient blackness, pierced here and there with a rayless star; taking the sweet air of the moors and the night into his bosom deeply; seeking, perhaps finding, peace after the manner of the unhappy. He turned round as she came in, and showed her a pale face against the window-frame.

"Is that you, Kirstie?" he asked. "Come in!"

page 144 / 166

"It's unco late, my dear," said Kirstie, affecting unwillingness.

"No, no," he answered, "not at all. Come in, if you want a crack. I am not sleepy, God knows!"

She advanced, took a chair by the toilet table and the candle, and set the rushlight at her foot. Something - it might be in the comparative disorder of her dress, it might be the emotion that now welled in her bosom - had touched her with a wand of transformation, and she seemed young with the youth of goddesses.

"Mr. Erchie," she began, "what's this that's come to ye?"

"I am not aware of anything that has come," said Archie, and blushed, and repented bitterly that he had let her in.

"O, my dear, that'll no dae!" said Kirstie. "It's ill to blend the eyes of love. O, Mr. Erchie, tak a thocht ere it's ower late. Ye shouldna be impatient o' the braws o' life, they'll a' come in their saison, like the sun and the rain. Ye're young yet; ye've mony cantie years afore ye. See and dinna wreck yersel' at the outset like sae mony ithers!

Hae patience - they telled me aye that was the owercome o' life - hae patience, there's a braw day coming yet. Gude kens it never cam to me; and here I am, wi' nayther man nor bairn to ca' my ain, wearying a'

folks wi' my ill tongue, and you just the first, Mr. Erchie!"

"I have a difficulty in knowing what you mean," said Archie.

"Weel, and I'll tell ye," she said. "It's just this, that I'm feared.

I'm feared for ye, my dear. Remember, your faither is a hard man, reaping where he hasna sowed and gaithering where he hasna strawed.

It's easy speakin', but mind! Ye'll have to look in the gurly face o'm, where it's ill to look, and vain to look for mercy. Ye mind me o' a bonny ship pitten oot into the black and gowsty seas - ye're a' safe still, sittin' quait and crackin' wi' Kirstie in your lown chalmer; but whaur will ye be the morn, and in whatten horror o' the fearsome tempest, cryin' on the hills to cover ye?"

"Why, Kirstie, you're very enigmatical to-night - and very eloquent,"

Archie put in.

"And, my dear Mr. Erchie," she continued, with a change of voice, "ye mauna think that I canna sympathise wi' ye. Ye mauna think that I havena been young mysel'. Lang syne, when I was a bit lassie, no twenty yet - " She paused and sighed. "Clean and caller, wi' a fit like the hinney bee," she continned. "I was aye big and buirdly, ye maun understand; a bonny figure o' a woman, though I say it that suldna -

built to rear bairns - braw bairns they suld hae been, and grand I would hae likit it! But I was young, dear, wi' the bonny glint o' youth in my e'en, and little I dreamed I'd ever be tellin' ye this, an auld, lanely, rudas wife! Weel, Mr. Erchie, there was a lad cam' courtin' me, as was page 146 / 166

but naetural. Mony had come before, and I would nane o' them. But this yin had a tongue to wile the birds frae the lift and the bees frae the foxglove bells. Deary me, but it's lang syne! Folk have dee'd sinsyne and been buried, and are forgotten, and bairns been born and got merrit and got bairns o' their ain. Sinsyne woods have been plantit, and have grawn up and are bonny trees, and the joes sit in their shadow, and sinsyne auld estates have changed hands, and there have been wars and rumours of wars on the face of the earth. And here I'm still - like an auld droopit craw - lookin' on and craikin'! But, Mr. Erchie, do ye no think that I have mind o' it a' still? I was dwalling then in my faither's house; and it's a curious thing that we were whiles trysted in the Deil's Hags. And do ye no think that I have mind of the bonny simmer days, the lang miles o' the bluid-red heather, the cryin' of the whaups, and the lad and the lassie that was trysted? Do ye no think that I mind how the hilly sweetness ran about my hairt? Ay, Mr. Erchie, I ken the way o' it - fine do I ken the way - how the grace o' God takes them, like Paul of Tarsus, when they think it least, and drives the pair o' them into a land which is like a dream, and the world and the folks in't' are nae mair than clouds to the puir lassie, and heeven nae mair than windle-straes, if she can but pleesure him! Until Tam dee'd - that was my story," she broke off to say, "he dee'd, and I wasna at the buryin'. But while he was here, I could take care o' mysel'. And can yon puir lassie?"

Kirstie, her eyes shining with unshed tears, stretched out her hand towards him appealingly; the bright and the dull gold of her hair flashed and smouldered in the coils behind her comely head, like the page 147 / 166

rays of an eternal youth; the pure colour had risen in her face; and Archie was abashed alike by her beauty and her story. He came towards her slowly from the window, took up her hand in his and kissed it.

"Kirstie," he said hoarsely, "you have misjudged me sorely. I have always thought of her, I wouldna harm her for the universe, my woman!"

"Eh, lad, and that's easy sayin'," cried Kirstie, "but it's nane sae easy doin'! Man, do ye no comprehend that it's God's wull we should be blendit and glamoured, and have nae command over our ain members at a time like that? My bairn," she cried, still holding his hand, "think o'

the puir lass! have pity upon her, Erchie! and O, be wise for twa!

Think o' the risk she rins! I have seen ye, and what's to prevent ithers! I saw ye once in the Hags, in my ain howl, and I was wae to see ye there - in pairt for the omen, for I think there's a weird on the place - and in pairt for pure nakit envy and bitterness o' hairt. It's strange ye should forgather there tae! God! but yon puir, thrawn, auld Covenanter's seen a heap o' human natur since he lookit his last on the musket barrels, if he never saw nane afore," she added, with a kind of wonder in her eyes.

"I swear by my honour I have done her no wrong," said Archie. "I swear by my honour and the redemption of my soul that there shall none be done her. I have heard of this before. I have been foolish, Kirstie, not unkind, and, above all, not base."

page 148 / 166

"There's my bairn!" said Kirstie, rising. "I'll can trust ye noo, I'll can gang to my bed wi' an easy hairt." And then she saw in a flash how barren had been her triumph. Archie had promised to spare the girl, and he would keep it; but who had promised to spare Archie? What was to be the end of it? Over a maze of difficulties she glanced, and saw, at the end of every passage, the flinty countenance of Hermiston. And a kind of horror fell upon her at what she had done. She wore a tragic mask.

"Erchie, the Lord peety you, dear, and peety me! I have buildit on this foundation" - laying her hand heavily on his shoulder - "and buildit hie, and pit my hairt in the buildin' of it. If the hale hypothec were to fa', I think, laddie, I would dee! Excuse a daft wife that loves ye, and that kenned your mither. And for His name's sake keep yersel' frae inordinate desires; haud your heart in baith your hands, carry it canny and laigh; dinna send it up like a hairn's kite into the collieshangic o' the wunds! Mind, Maister Erchie dear, that this life's a'

disappointment, and a mouthfu' o' mools is the appointed end."

"Ay, but Kirstie, my woman, you're asking me ower much at last," said Archie, profoundly moved, and lapsing into the broad Scots. "Ye're asking what nae man can grant ye, what only the Lord of heaven can grant ye if He see fit. Ay! And can even He! I can promise ye what I shall do, and you can depend on that. But how I shall feel - my woman, that is long past thinking of!"

They were both standing by now opposite each other. The face of Archie wore the wretched semblance of a smile; hers was convulsed for a moment.

"Promise me ae thing," she cried in a sharp voice. "Promise me ye'll never do naething without telling me."

"No, Kirstie, I canna promise ye that," he replied. "I have promised enough, God kens!"

"May the blessing of God lift and rest upon ye dear!" she said.

"God bless ye, my old friend," said he.

CHAPTER IX - AT THE WEAVER'S STONE

IT was late in the afternoon when Archie drew near by the hill path to the Praying Weaver's stone. The Hags were in shadow. But still, through the gate of the Slap, the sun shot a last arrow, which sped far and straight across the surface of the moss, here and there touching and shining on a tussock, and lighted at length on the gravestone and the small figure awaiting him there. The emptiness and solitude of the great moors seemed to be concentrated there, and Kirstie pointed out by that figure of sunshine for the only inhabitant. His first sight of her was thus excruciatingly sad, like a glimpse of a world from which all light, comfort, and society were on the point of vanishing. And the next moment, when she had turned her face to him and the quick smile had enlightened it, the whole face of nature smiled upon him in her smile of page 150 / 166

welcome. Archie's slow pace was quickened; his legs hasted to her though his heart was hanging back. The girl, upon her side, drew herself together slowly and stood up, expectant; she was all languor, her face was gone white; her arms ached for him, her soul was on tip-toes. But he deceived her, pausing a few steps away, not less white than herself, and holding up his hand with a gesture of denial.

"No, Christina, not to-day," he said. "To-day I have to talk to you seriously. Sit ye down, please, there where you were. Please!" he repeated.

The revulsion of feeling in Christina's heart was violent. To have longed and waited these weary hours for him, rehearsing her endearments

- to have seen him at last come - to have been ready there, breathless, wholly passive, his to do what he would with - and suddenly to have found herself confronted with a grey-faced, harsh schoolmaster - it was too rude a shock. She could have wept, but pride withheld her. She sat down on the stone, from which she had arisen, part with the instinct of obedience, part as though she had been thrust there. What was this?

Why was she rejected? Had she ceased to please? She stood here offering her wares, and he would none of them! And yet they were all his! His to take and keep, not his to refuse though! In her quick petulant nature, a moment ago on fire with hope, thwarted love and wounded vanity wrought. The schoolmaster that there is in all men, to the despair of all girls and most women, was now completely in possession of Archie. He had passed a night of sermons, a day of reflection; he had come wound up to do his duty; and the set mouth, page 151 / 166

which in him only betrayed the effort of his will, to her seemed the expression of an averted heart. It was the same with his constrained voice and embarrassed utterance; and if so - if it was all over - the pang of the thought took away from her the power of thinking.

He stood before her some way off. "Kirstie, there's been too much of this. We've seen too much of each other." She looked up quickly and her eyes contracted. "There's no good ever comes of these secret meetings. They're not frank, not honest truly, and I ought to have seen it. People have begun to talk; and it's not right of me. Do you see?"

"I see somebody will have been talking to ye," she said sullenly.

"They have, more than one of them," replied Archie.

"And whae were they?" she cried. "And what kind o' love do ye ca' that, that's ready to gang round like a whirligig at folk talking? Do ye think they havena talked to me?"

"Have they indeed?" said Archie, with a quick breath. "That is what I feared. Who were they? Who has dared - ?"

Archie was on the point of losing his temper.

page 152 / 166

As a matter of fact, not any one had talked to Christina on the matter; and she strenuously repeated her own first question in a panic of self-defence.

"Ah, well! what does it matter?" he said. "They were good folk that wished well to us, and the great affair is that there are people talking. My dear girl, we have to be wise. We must not wreck our lives at the outset. They may be long and happy yet, and we must see to it, Kirstie, like God's rational creatures and not like fool children.

There is one thing we must see to before all. You're worth waiting for, Kirstie! worth waiting for a generation; it would be enough reward." -

And here he remembered the schoolmaster again, and very unwisely took to following wisdom. "The first thing that we must see to, is that there shall be no scandal about for my father's sake. That would ruin all; do ye no see that?"

Kirstie was a little pleased, there had been some show of warmth of sentiment in what Archie had said last. But the dull irritation still persisted in her bosom; with the aboriginal instinct, having suffered herself, she wished to make Archie suffer.

And besides, there had come out the word she had always feared to hear from his lips, the name of his father. It is not to be supposed that, during so many days with a love avowed between them, some reference had not been made to their conjoint future. It had in fact been often touched upon, and from the first had been the sore point. Kirstie had page 153 / 166

wilfully closed the eye of thought; she would not argue even with herself; gallant, desperate little heart, she had accepted the command of that supreme attraction like the call of fate and marched blindfold on her doom. But Archie, with his masculine sense of responsibility, must reason; he must dwell on some future good, when the present good was all in all to Kirstie; he must talk - and talk lamely, as necessity drove him - of what was to be. Again and again he had touched on marriage; again and again been driven back into indistinctness by a memory of Lord Hermiston. And Kirstie had been swift to understand and quick to choke down and smother the understanding; swift to leap up in flame at a mention of that hope, which spoke volumes to her vanity and her love, that she might one day be Mrs. Weir of Hermiston; swift, also, to recognise in his stumbling or throttled utterance the death-knell of these expectations, and constant, poor girl! in her large-minded madness, to go on and to reck nothing of the future. But these unfinished references, these blinks in which his heart spoke, and his memory and reason rose up to silence it before the words were well uttered, gave her unqualifiable agony. She was raised up and dashed down again bleeding. The recurrence of the subject forced her, for however short a time, to open her eyes on what she did not wish to see; and it had invariably ended in another disappointment. So now again, at the mere wind of its coming, at the mere mention of his father's name -

who might seem indeed to have accompanied them in their whole moorland courtship, an awful figure in a wig with an ironical and bitter smile, present to guilty consciousness - she fled from it head down.

"Ye havena told me yet," she said, "who was it spoke?"

"Your aunt for one," said Archie.

"Auntie Kirstie?" she cried. "And what do I care for my Auntie Kirstie?"

"She cares a great deal for her niece," replied Archie, in kind reproof.

"Troth, and it's the first I've heard of it," retorted the girl.

"The question here is not who it is, but what they say, what they have noticed," pursued the lucid schoolmaster. "That is what we have to think of in self-defence."

"Auntie Kirstie, indeed! A bitter, thrawn auld maid that's fomented trouble in the country before I was born, and will be doing it still, I daur say, when I'm deid! It's in her nature; it's as natural for her as it's for a sheep to eat."

"Pardon me, Kirstie, she was not the only one," interposed Archie. "I had two warnings, two sermons, last night, both most kind and considerate. Had you been there, I promise you you would have grat, my dear! And they opened my eyes. I saw we were going a wrong way."

"Who was the other one?" Kirstie demanded.

By this time Archie was in the condition of a hunted beast. He had come, braced and resolute; he was to trace out a line of conduct for the pair of them in a few cold, convincing sentences; he had now been there some time, and he was still staggering round the outworks and undergoing what he felt to be a savage cross-examination.

"Mr. Frank!" she cried. "What nex', I would like to ken?"

"He spoke most kindly and truly."

"What like did he say?"

"I am not going to tell you; you have nothing to do with that," cried Archie, startled to find he had admitted so much.

"O, I have naething to do with it!" she repeated, springing to her feet.

"A'body at Hermiston's free to pass their opinions upon me, but I have naething to do wi' it! Was this at prayers like? Did ye ca' the grieve into the consultation? Little wonder if a'body's talking, when ye make a'body yer confidants! But as you say, Mr. Weir, - most kindly, most considerately, most truly, I'm sure, - I have naething to do with it.

And I think I'll better be going. I'll be wishing you good evening, Mr.

Weir." And she made him a stately curtsey, shaking as she did so from head to foot, with the barren ecstasy of temper.

Poor Archie stood dumbfounded. She had moved some steps away from him before he recovered the gift of articulate speech.

"Kirstie!" he cried. "O, Kirstie woman!"

There was in his voice a ring of appeal, a clang of mere astonishment that showed the schoolmaster was vanquished.

She turned round on him. "What do ye Kirstie me for?" she retorted.

"What have ye to do wi' me! Gang to your ain freends and deave them!"

He could only repeat the appealing "Kirstie!"

"Kirstie, indeed!" cried the girl, her eyes blazing in her white face.

"My name is Miss Christina Elliott, I would have ye to ken, and I daur ye to ca' me out of it. If I canna get love, I'll have respect, Mr.

Weir. I'm come of decent people, and I'll have respect. What have I done that ye should lightly me? What have I done? What have I done?

O, what have I done?" and her voice rose upon the third repetition. "I thocht - I thocht - I thocht I was sae happy!"

and the first sob broke from her like the paroxysm of some mortal sickness.

Archie ran to her. He took the poor child in his arms, and she nestled to his breast as to a mother's, and clasped him in hands that were strong like vices. He felt her whole body shaken by the throes of distress, and had pity upon her beyond speech. Pity, and at the same time a bewildered fear of this explosive engine in his arms, whose works he did not understand, and yet had been tampering with. There arose from before him the curtains of boyhood, and he saw for the first time the ambiguous face of woman as she is. In vain he looked back over the interview; he saw not where he had offended. It seemed unprovoked, a wilful convulsion of brute nature. . . .

GLOSSARY

Ae, one.

Antinomian, one of a sect which holds that under the gospel dispensation the moral law is not obligatory.

Auld Hornie, the Devil.

Ballant, ballad.

Bauchles, brogues, old shoes.

Bauld, bold.

Bees in their bonnet, eccentricities.

Birling, whirling.

Black-a-vised, dark-complexioned.

Bonnet-laird, small landed proprietor, yeoman.

Bool, ball.

Brae, rising ground.

Brig, bridge.

Buff, play buff on, to make a fool of, to deceive.

Burn, stream.

Butt end, end of a cottage.

Byre, cow-house.

Ca', drive.

Caller, fresh.

Canna, cannot.

Canny, careful, shrewd.

Cantie, cheerful.

Carline, old woman.

Cauld, cold.

Chalmer, chamber.

Claes, clothes.

Clamjamfry, crowd.

Clavers, idle talk.

Cock-laird. See Bonnet-laird.

Collieshangie, turmoil.

Crack, to converse.

Cuist, cast.

Cuddy, donkey.

Cutty, jade, also used playfully = brat.

Daft, mad, frolicsome.

page 159 / 166

Dander, to saunter.

Danders, cinders.

Daurna, dare not.

Deave, to deafen.

Denty, dainty.

Dirdum, vigour.

Disjaskit, worn out, disreputable-looking.

Doer, law agent.

Dour, hard.

Drumlie, dark.

Dunting, knocking.

Dwaibly, infirm, rickety.

Dule-tree, the tree of lamentation, the hanging-tree.

Earrand, errand.

Ettercap, vixen.

Fechting, fighting.

Feck, quantity, portion.

Feckless, feeble, powerless.

Fell, strong and fiery.

Fey, unlike yourself, strange, as if urged on by fate, or as persons are observed to be in the hour of approaching death or disaster.

Fit, foot.

Flit, to depart.

Flyped, turned up, turned in-side out.

Forbye, in addition to.

page 160 / 166

Forgather, to fall in with.

Fower, four.

Fushionless, pithless, weak.

Fyle, to soil, to defile.

Fylement, obloquy, defilement.

Gaed, Went.

Gang, to go.

Gey an', very.

Gigot, leg of mutton.

Girzie, lit. diminutive of Grizel, here a playful nickname.

Glaur, mud.

Glint, glance, sparkle.

Gloaming, twilight.

Glower, to scowl.

Gobbets, small lumps.

Gowden, golden.

Gowsty, gusty.

Grat, wept.

Grieve, land-steward.

Guddle, to catch fish with the hands by groping under the stones or banks.

Gumption, common sense, judgment.

Guid, good.

Gurley, stormy, surly.

Gyte, beside itself.

Hae, have, take.

Haddit, held.

Hale, whole.

Heels-ower-hurdie, heels over head.

Hinney, honey.

Hirstle, to bustle.

Hizzie, wench.

Howe, hollow.

Howl, hovel.

Hunkered, crouched.

Hypothec, lit. in Scots law the furnishings of a house, and formerly the produce and stock of a farm hypothecated by law to the landlord as security for rent; colloquially "the whole structure," "the whole concern."

Idleset, idleness.

Infeftment, a term in Scots law originally synonymous with investiture.

Jaud, jade.

Jeely-piece, a slice of bread and jelly.

Jennipers, juniper.

Jo, sweetheart.

Justifeed, executed, made the victim of justice.

Jyle, jail

page 162 / 166

Kebbuck, cheese.

Ken, to know.

Kenspeckle, conspicuous.

Kilted, tucked up.

Kyte, belly.

Laigh, low.

Laird, landed proprietor.

Lane, alone.

Lave, rest, remainder.

Linking, tripping.

Lown, lonely, still.

Lynn, cataract.

Lyon King of Arms, the chief of the Court of Heraldry in Scotland.

Macers, offiers of the supreme court. [Cf. Guy Mannering, last chapter.]

Maun, must.

Menseful, of good manners.

Mirk, dark.

Misbegowk, deception, disappointment.

Mools, mould, earth.

Muckle, much, great, big.

My lane, by myself.

Nowt, black cattle.

Palmering, walking infirmly.

Panel, in Scots law, the accused person in a criminal action, the prisoner.

Peel, fortified watch-tower.

Plew-stilts, plough-handles.

Policy, ornamental grounds of a country mansion.

Puddock, frog.

Quean, wench.

Rair, to roar.

Riff-raff, rabble.

Risping, grating.

Rout, rowt, to roar, to rant.

Rowth, abundance.

Rudas, haggard old woman.

Runt, an old cow past breeding; opprobriously, an old woman.

Sab, sob.

Sanguishes, sandwiches.

Sasine, in Scots law, the act of giving legal possession of feudal property, or, colloquially, the deed by which that possession is proved.

Sclamber, to scramble.

Sculduddery, impropriety, grossness.

page 164 / 166

Session, the Court of Session, the supreme court of Scotland.

Shauchling, shuffling, slipshod.

Shoo, to chase gently.

Siller, money.

Sinsyne, since then.

Skailing, dispersing.

Skelp, slap.

Skirling, screaming.

Skriegh-o'day, daybreak.

Snash, abuse.

Sneisty, supercilious.

Sooth, to hum.

Sough, sound, murmur.

Spec, The Speculative Society, a debating Society connected with Edingburgh University.

Speir, to ask.

Speldering, sprawling.

Splairge, to splash.

Spunk, spirit, fire.

Steik, to shut.

Stockfish, hard, savourless.

Suger-bool, suger-plum.

Syne, since, then.

Tawpie, a slow foolish slut, also used playfully = monkey.

Telling you, a good thing for you.

Thir, these.

Thrawn, cross-grained.

Toon, town.

Two-names, local soubriquets in addition to patronymic.

Tyke, dog.

Unchancy, unlucky.

Unco, strange, extraordinary, very.

Upsitten, impertinent.

Vennel, alley, lane. The Vennel, a narrow lane in Edingburgh, running out of the Grassmarket.

Vivers, victuals.

Wae, sad, unhappy.

Waling, choosing.

Warrandise, warranty.

Waur, worse.

Weird, destiny.

Whammle, to upset.

Whaup, curlew.

Whiles, sometimes.

Windlestae, crested dog's-tail, grass.

Wund, wind.

page 166 / 166

Printed in Great Britain
by Amazon